SEAN M.

There Are Few Who Can Bear It

Book 3 of the
Whim-Dark Tales

sean@seanmts.com
FIRST EDITION
www.seanmts.com
Edited by the Ebook Launch Team.
Cover design by Miblart.

Table of Contents

Part I: The Knights Cosmic

Wundan pressed himself against the coarse bark of a mighty steel oak. With every exhale his cheek puffed against the cracks in the bark that gripped and scratched at his flesh. He held his breath, stifling the sounds of his being as the crell birds sang, their dulcet chimes cascading throughout the glen.

The pleasant cacophony of the woods consumed him as he tried to ignore the thrumming in his ears and the rising pressure in his lungs.

A twig snapped somewhere close. He resisted the urge to gasp and twitch, not daring to make a noise.

"Wundan?" The voice was a harsh whisper, full of doubt.

Wundan smirked. Crateon had no idea he was here. With a shout he sprang from his hiding place and barrelled into the youngling orc that was stalking him. "Huzzah!" The two boys tumbled through the undergrowth, laughing as they tried to pin one another to the ground.

"Damnations, you humans are too sneaky!" Crateon struck Wundan across the jaw. Wundan grunted and tumbled off so that the orc could gain the upper hand in the brawl. "Pinned, give up, pinky!"

"No fair!" Wundan spat out a mouthful of dirt and blood. "We said no punching!"

"I didn't punch you! I hit you!"

"Same thing!"

"Is not!"

"Bah!" Wundan relaxed, resigning to the hold Crateon had on him. "Fine, you win!"

Crateon chirped and roared—to the dismay of the crell birds that fluttered away with squawks of alarm. After relishing in his victory—and once the crell birds settled to resume their song—he hefted Wundan up. "Now you owe my village one of your chickens."

"Mother won't be happy with that," Wundan grumbled.

"Then you shouldn't have made the bet, pinky. If you wanted to get one of my father's piglets, you should have been stronger."

"I'll be stronger." Wundan shoved Crateon. "Don't you worry about that, tusk face."

"Now don't be mean . . ." Crateon made to shove back when he suddenly went quiet, his muscles going tense.

"What, got no comeback?" Wundan laughed.

"Shh." Crateon grabbed Wundan by the shoulders and shoved him back down into the undergrowth.

"Hey, I said you won, hey . . ." Crateon muffled Wundan's voice by shoving his lightly scaled hand over his mouth.

"Something's wrong," Crateon said. "The crell stopped singing."

Wundan ripped Crateon's hand from his mouth. "You scared them off."

"They settled down afterwards, and they haven't flown off this time. They've gone quiet." The two boys waited in the undergrowth, listening in the now silent forest. Crateon's nostrils flared. "I smell smoke."

"I smell something else," Wundan gasped, his nostrils rankled. "Smells like rotting crops."

The boys locked eyes as the setting dread pulled them closer to the soil.

"You don't suppose it's carrites?" Crateon asked.

"Carrites only creep in to feed in the wake of raided villages, dead bodies and all that. Though, my village is the closest, and I haven't heard no warning bells."

A low, clicking growl interrupted them, sending chills down their spines. Something rustled in the brush.

Crateon eyed Wundan. "They could be anticipating bloodshed."

"But that would mean . . . they think one of our villages is about to get raided?" Wundan said.

"We need to warn them," Crateon said.

"They won't believe us," Wundan protested. "I'm not even allowed to be out here alone!"

The clicking growl grew closer.

"Shh," Crateon growled himself and pointed through the undergrowth. "I see it."

Wundan squinted along the line of Crateon's finger and saw a creature with ragged fur slink around a tree and out of sight. It had gleaming red eyes and claws of granite.

"That is a carrite!" Wundan's voice cracked and he started panting.

"Look." Crateon pulled him close. "They eat bodies, not living people. We need to make a break for it to warn our villages."

"Yeah, but I'm sure they'll like munching on a little boy once in a while!"

"Wundan!" Crateon growled lower. "Our families are in danger. Think of your mother."

Wundan bit down on his fears. He had to be strong, for Mum. "Okay, on three, we up and leg it."

Crateon nodded. "One." He tensed.

"Two." Wundan tried not to think about the sick feeling about to spew from his guts.

The clicking growl peaked as the carrite slunk back around the tree and glanced in their direction.

"Three!" The orc and human boy upped and bolted from cover, splitting up and startling the carrite.

Wundan didn't look back as he stormed through the foliage, tearing down the hill towards his village on the outskirts of the forest. He didn't falter as the clicking growl followed in his wake. But he did pale when his village's warning bell rang out across the glen . . .

Twenty Years Later

The tips of dead tree branches tore at Seria's face as she sped through the swamp. The horrible creature crashed through gnarled roots and dredged up the foul-smelling bog in her wake.

Light and nimble, she scurried up a log and leaped from tree to tree, protecting herself from being caught in the treacherous waters and keeping one step ahead of the creature.

But it was catching up.

Her robes caught in the skeletal fingers of a half-submerged mangrove and halted her momentum. "Fuck!"

She spun as an enormous, insidious maw loomed to engulf her *and* the entire tree she was caught in. Its jaws opened like the bloom of a demented flower, revealing a conduit into the black abyss within that was lined with row upon row of razor-sharp teeth. The stench of rot and bile assailed her, and she scrunched her face in revulsion.

She made a motion with her arms, as if lashing out at the beast. With a bubbling hiss the waters of the swamp surged upwards at her command and whipped the grotesque creature across what passed for a face. With a howl it stumbled back into the darkness.

Seria was a nymph, small and blue-skinned with flowing hair that resembled dark green seaweed. When this thing attacked her commune, she drew it away into the dead swamps. She alone took on this burden, because out of all the nymphs in her city, she had the one advantage over them to help her defeat this creature.

She did not care about abusing her sacred power in order to kill a beast when it asked for it. The rest of the nymphs vowed only to defend, and that's why many of them were now dead. This creature grew with every kill, the nymphs' essence siphoned into its very being. But Seria was not about to let that continue.

She watched with a satisfied grin as the beast lurched back in pain; then she whipped a lashing of water to slice the dead fingers of the tree that gripped at her, and she fell into the churning swamp with a plop. Her feet sank into the bog until she was waist deep. But that did not matter to her; this would be where she made her last stand.

The hulking creature staggered in the mush until it righted itself. It was unidentifiable, with gelatinous grey skin that churned and frothed and folded in on itself like the raging seas. It was like a great slug with random, spindly, sharp spider limbs protruding from it at every angle at irregular intervals. It turned to leer down at its defiant victim.

Something flickered deep within Seria as she met its gaze, a spark, fleeting but powerful. She gasped, "What was that?" but she did not have time to dwell on the strange sensation, as the thing was poised to strike. "Come on!" she challenged, biting back the sudden fear that surged in her throat. *This might have been a mistake, but it was me or my commune.* "Come on, you bastard!"

Letting out a deep, rumbling roar, the creature descended upon her. With a twist of her body and limbs, the waters swirled about Seria and channelled into the beast as a mighty blast of pressure. The swamp surged toward Seria and her spell like a whirlpool before jetting into her enemy in a continuous stream.

The foul creature roared and pressed against her attack even as she summoned more water to her cause. The two struggled, locked in a battle of wills, and the coursing waters lowered around Seria's legs. She could not keep this up for long.

The hulking horror ducked to the side and tore down the edge of the jet stream to swipe at Seria. She twisted again and lashed the last of her power downwards, whipping the waters to smash her enemy into the rapidly draining swamp. Mud splashed up into her face and stung her eyes. She cried out and slipped back into the bog with a squelch.

The creature reared as the putrid water rained back down around them, and it bore down to feast on her bones.

Before she could scream, before she could cover her blurred vision in order to avoid witnessing her dreadful fate, there was a flash of bright, colourful light and then a titanic boom.

The creature roared as it stumbled back, and Seria blinked away the mud and disbelief. Before her stood a knight, bristling in technicoloured plate armour, who took up a position between her and the monster.

In his hands he held a war hammer of silver that pulsed and shone as he did. The creature reared to strike him, but there was another explosion of coloured light, and another, and another. A whole squadron of knights streaked down from the star-scattered sky and struck at the beast with weapons of brilliant light and power.

The first to arrive turned to her as his comrades engaged the creature in a brawl of stellar brilliance. His armour flashed with bright, cascading, ethereal colours, as if someone was pouring liquid light over him from above. The plate was almost translucent, revealing hints of the warrior beneath it, with rippling, furry muscles and a smile beneath the visor that revealed sharp fangs.

"Are you well, maiden?" His voice was deep and rough.

"Who are you?" Seria said.

A knight using his shield as a bludgeon leaped onto the creature and clobbered it from above.

"I am Sir Rorc." He lifted his visor, revealing the head of a lion that flashed its teeth with a cheeky grin. "And we are the Knights Cosmic."

"Rorc, you bastard!" one of his comrades bellowed with a guttural sound. "A little help!"

"Yeah, *Captain*! What was that talk about teamwork, and leading from the front?" another of his comrades hissed. Their voice was harsh and wispy at the same time; it came from a knight that had many legs and two curved fangs protruding from its visor.

Rorc grunted, "Scuse me, ma'am, but they have a point." He flicked his visor closed with a nod and turned to the fray, hefting the silver hammer, which was almost as tall as he was.

With a roar that made Seria flinch, the lion knight Sir Rorc catapulted himself from the muddy mound and struck the hideous creature into the marshy landscape. It bellowed a pained moan and lashed out in response with unseemly, wiry limbs that resembled the dead tree branches around the swamp. The nightmarish limbs raked against the Knights Cosmic, scraping upon their technicoloured armour with great sparks that knocked the warriors back. But each blow failed to kill or maim, and the integrity of the strange plate held even against the might of the foul beast.

Every time they were knocked back, the knights picked themselves out from the swamp with an agility that belied the weight of their armour and weapons. They kept converging on the withering creature with the sheer resolve of an inevitable victory.

Seria watched in awe as the squadron fought the beast with a fury that matched its terror; they assisted one another without hesitation and with a litany of jovial banter. While the battle raged, her eye was drawn to one particular knight who fought with sword and shield and maintained a stoic silence in comparison to the banter of his friends. As he struck at the beast, his cry was more bloodcurdling than the lion knight Rorc's. When his comrades were knocked back, he would throw his body between them and the pressing strike of the beast, and then retaliate with a ferocity that would make the embodiment of rage tremble in fear.

After weathering an ungodly assault from the Knights Cosmic for so long, the creature cried out and launched its mass of twisting, wiry limbs into the swamp. It burrowed itself into the murky, half-solid depths.

The silence was palpable. The trembling earth dwindled to stillness, punctuated only by the breathless knights trying to regroup.

Seria broke the quiet. "A whole division of nymphs who hailed from fire, stone, and water failed to even make that creature flinch. What are the Knights Cosmic, to make it flee?"

The hulking knight that had a voice gruffer than Rorc's swaggered up to her. "Ah, but more impressively, who are you, to stand alone and keep the creature at bay for so long?"

"I am Seria Wish of Marsil. And you are?"

The knight dropped his war hammer—a smaller affair compared to his captain's—and removed his helmet to reveal an ape-looking creature with a mischievous grin. "I am Sir Rafek Gauntlet, at your service, ma'am." He made a show of bowing low.

With the top-heavy nature of his hulking arms and torso, compared to his relatively skinny legs, it seemed he might topple face first into the slowly refilling swamps, but his balance held.

"Rafek, the battle isn't over yet," the stoic knight said sternly. "Banter comes afterwards."

"Of course, Sir Drade." Rafek winked at Seria and donned his helmet. "He's always so serious when he channels Prismatic Plate."

"Prismatic what?"

But Seria's question went unanswered as the swamps bubbled and the earth trembled. The beast burst forth from the depths, larger and more terrifying than before and pulsing with green, *necromantic* light.

"Fuck me! Where did those souls come from?" the multi-armed knight hissed and skittered away like a spider.

All the knights were knocked from their feet and smacked down into the bog by the exploding earth and the now thicker limbs of the emerging beast—all the knights save for Sir Rorc and Sir Drade.

The beast towered into the air with a body thick and slimy like a slug's, and it twisted, weaving its limbs around it like dancing blades that whistled in the air. It formed a razor-sharp spinning point at its head that swivelled and bore down to drill through the lion knight.

Rorc roared and conjured a shield of prismatic essence. It winked into existence, cascading outwards from his very heart, appearing like a rainbow after a storm. He braced himself for the attack as Drade packed in behind him, placing his arm on the pulsing shield and adding his power to Rorc's. The shield shone brilliantly and grew in thickness, twice as strong, three times, four, before the beast's drilling body slammed into it.

The spinning point of the creature with its whole mass behind it drove against the mighty shield that the two knights conjured as they held their ground. The creature screeched and drove harder, mud and bog and decaying matter flung in every direction as it spun, as if a hurricane raged through the battlefield. The knights roared and hunkered down. The titanic struggle of wills ended when the shield cracked like glass. There was an explosion of colour that blinded Seria from seeing the outcome.

Dazed, she blinked away the stars from her vision and found Sir Rorc pinned halfway up a gnarled tree, with several of the beast's limbs skewering through his torso, leg, and neck. He gurgled, his head turning to look into the monstrous, gaping jaws that towered over him.

A grunt of pain drew her attention further down the tree where Sir Drade was pinned by his shoulder, a spindly limb skewering his pauldron. His face was obscured by the shimmering, technicoloured helm. But Seria could tell from the way he glanced between the creature and his skewered captain that a rage dwarfing his previous display was building.

The other knights were still recovering. It was up to Drade.

Drade's plate armour flared bright. The creature screeched as the limb skewering him was burned at the pauldron and snapped off. Drade stumbled to his knees and grabbed for his sword. The weapon responded to his call—flicking into his grip—and he launched from the ground like a streaking comet, slamming into the beast's head. He swung his silver sword with a mighty arc that cleaved through sinister flesh and bone. He burst through the other side of the creature, having decapitated the thing with one fell swipe. His streaking path arched down into the swamp, and he landed with a plop as the twitching, writhing body of his enemy crashed into the ground. It released its hold on the dying captain, who fell into the arms of the monkey knight, Rafek.

The creature writhed and crumbled into ashes. Drade picked himself up from the muck to stalk back to Rorc as the squadron congregated around him.

Despite her more timid instincts begging her not to, Seria crept over to their vigil. "Is he . . ."

"Yes." Drade grunted. "My power was only enough to avenge him, not to protect him."

"Do not be too hard on yourself, brother." Rafek laid his captain down against the tree as the other knights whispered their respects and held his armoured paws. "Now his duty is done; his soul can finally return to the sun of his people and be at peace."

"I guess so." Drade didn't move a muscle as Rafek placed his mighty palm on his wounded shoulder and cocked his head with concern. "My powers will heal it soon like all the rest," Drade answered the unasked question.

"I am not worried about your physical ailment," Rafek replied.

Drade's helmet shifted to regard his friend. He gave a slight nod and went back to watch over the captain, who spluttered and gasped his last.

"You can let go now, Captain," the multi-limbed knight hissed.

"Be with your people," another knight with a scaly tail and a snouted helm whispered gently.

The captain sighed and his body went limp.

"I'm sorry," Seria said. "He died to save me. I'm sorry."

"Not just you, Seria of Marsil," Rafek hummed, "but a great many souls, all as worthy as the rest. Now watch, his armour shall carry him home."

The prismatic plate shimmered; polyps of silver light rose from the surface and then seeped back through the cracks and rents in the armour, into the lion's flesh.

"May his soul shine brightly upon the cosmos," Drade murmured.

"As his duty allowed others to pass on in peace," the knights chanted like a prayer. "His time has now come to rest."

The shimmering intensified, Rorc's body shuddered, and then the light waned and winked out.

The knights collectively cocked their heads.

"Arachton, is he still alive?" Drade asked.

The multi-limbed knight leaned in closer and shook his head. "No, he is gone."

"Why has his armour gone dark? Why has his soul not acquiesced as all knights are owed?" Drade growled.

"Is this not supposed to happen?" Seria asked.

"No." Drade turned and stalked away, regarding the churning ashes of the dying creature. His armour waned as he turned back to the group. "Something catastrophically fucked is happening. This Voir shouldn't have been able to ensnare the souls it did as it resurged. Something is catastrophically FUCKED!" His armour flickered and waned further. The translucent nature of the armour flared, revealing fragments of the man beneath.

"Easy, brother," Rafek growled. "Hone that rage to keep your armour intact. We are still exposed out here."

Drade sighed and his erratic demeanour calmed. His armour brightened and grew more opaque. "What about the girl? She has the fire."

"Yeah, little Seria, do you need an escort back to Marsil?" Rafek asked. "Or would you rather something else?"

Fire? Seria wondered. "Marsil is lost to me. The Council cast a spell to dissolve it into the sea miles away. It will reconstitute in time, but that could take decades, and it could take me decades more to find it . . . I am alone."

"Not exactly." Arachton skittered closer. "Any who can hold their own against the Voir must possess celestial fire."

Oh, fire. Seria shook her head with a laugh. "You mean paladism?" she scoffed. "I am no paladin."

"Paladism is a parlour trick compared to what the Knights Cosmic are capable of, ma'am." Drade stalked up to her. "You possess the celestial spark; it can summon prismatic fire. We all see it. With training you can bend it to your will in service of innocent souls that wander lost between the suns. If you wish, you can join us, and we will train you."

Seria regarded Drade for a long moment. "If I get to help people against those things, I will do anything you ask."

"Excellent attitude!" Rafek grinned and slapped her across the shoulder. "Now grip on tightly. You're about to experience what it's like to jettison across the universe!"

"I will bring Rorc's body." Drade knelt down and hefted the lion knight over his shoulders, gripping the war hammer under the nook of his arm. "The Roaming Wall is passing over us now."

The Squadron shimmered with technicoloured power as Seria gripped onto Rafek with all of her might. Then, with a blinding flash that mimicked their arrival, they jettisoned into the sky like streaking comets.

Seria was buffeted by icy winds, but the gentle heat of Rafek's technicoloured light warmed her. Those bodily sensations faded away, however, while Seria watched her blue-green world arch away from her as the horizons receded on all sides. The pillars of prismatic fire that the knights soared upon left streams of aurora in their wake, and she gasped in wonder. They ascended higher, until the clouds dissipated and the stars shone brighter than Seria could ever imagine. They sailed through the night sky, hurtling towards a floating fortress that drifted above it all.

It seemed like a castle at first glance, fierce and imposing. The structure looked as if it was torn from the ground and jettisoned into the heavens as a beacon of might. A bastion built from intricate blocks of blue-hued granite, with tiers of crenulated walls and turrets that sprouted from it in all directions to account for the three-dimensional assaults it must have endured. They hurtled towards a drawbridge built of oak and iron, which lowered itself into the void to welcome the approaching party.

With a yelp from Seria that made Rafek chuckle, they hurtled across the drawbridge and into the rapidly approaching gates. After she managed to pry her eyes open, Seria found herself still gripping onto Rafek with her head buried in his chest. They were standing in a great hall with a roaring fire, comfortable lounges, and a large dining table that stretched into the edges of the room. Pennants hung from the high ceilings which flew strange sigils and markings from a whole manner of different cultures. The walls were etched with designs of embossed precious metals depicting figures—some in silver who resembled the shape of the knights she now found herself with, and others in gold, who were tall and magnanimous.

"Welcome to the Roaming Wall," Rafek said as he pried her fingers from his chest. "It's one of the many Star Forts that drift across the cosmos." He allowed his armour to fade away, revealing a brown-furred ape with bulky arms and lean legs. He was wearing nothing but leather trousers, exposing his muscular chest, which was sparse of fur and covered in taut, leathery skin. "This is the common nexus." He gestured with his grey-skinned knuckles to the surrounding space. Gateways without doors stood against the walls beneath the embossed designs, revealing nothing but the bare stone in the walls behind them. "We are quite safe from any Voir here."

Seria silently took in the great hall as the other knights let their armour fade, revealing an eclectic mix of races and species, some of which she could not comprehend.

Besides Arachton—who was some kind of spider creature—there was a lizard man with red scales, a squat-looking human with brown skin and a black beard that reached to his knees, a muscled behemoth with light-yellow scales and tusks . . . and a human man, the one called Drade. He still held his dead captain in his arms. Even bearing the great weight of the lion knight in his armour—plus the war hammer—Drade stood as if he carried nothing.

Drade was unassuming, seeming like any of the humans who inhabited Seria's world. He was tall, broad, and possessed an agile look about him, even though he was rippling with musculature. He smiled at his companions, but his eyes remained stoic.

"Rafek, would you mind showing the new recruit the ropes while I report on Rorc's fate to the Knights Council?" Drade said.

"You taking over the squadron there, Drade?" the squat one with the beard asked.

"Fuck no, I'm recommending Rafek take over."

Seria wondered at the sudden change in him. Without his armour he seemed almost light-hearted . . . almost.

"That ape is too rash to lead," Arachton cut in, scuttling up to Rafek and Seria in a manner that made her skin crawl. "Look at his arms; they take all the blood supply from his brain."

"Does your kind even have a brain, bug?" Rafek squared up to the spider-thing. "Or is it just some weird nervous system designed to move in a way that gives me the creeps?"

"This should be good." The lizard man curled his tail around his waist and crossed his arms.

"Hey!" Drade's voice rose to a deafening bark. "We have bigger problems to worry about than your people's stupid blood feud!"

"She's just antsy 'cause I ate her eggs for breakfast, hmmm." Rafek rubbed his belly.

"You know my kind doesn't lay eggs!" Arachton reared, her legs waving in a threatening display as she bared her fangs. Her cluster of beady eyes fixated upon the monkey.

Seria glanced between the altercation and the other knights. The lizard and the other two were exchanging banter while Drade looked on with hopelessness, still cradling his dead captain. She remembered the way this spider and ape fought side by side not moments ago. *They must be reeling from their loss.* She had to help. These were her new comrades, after all.

"So, Arachton," she said, sidling between the ape and spider-thing, "your people are some sort of spider race, and you're named Arachton? Sounds a lot like arachnid."

Arachton stopped rearing and scuttled back a step, regarding Seria with her myriad of eyes.

"It's a nickname." Rafek sighed and his chest deflated from an intimidating display. "Most warm-blooded ape folk can't pronounce her name in her language."

"Not just the warm-bloods." The lizard man sniggered.

"So, what is it?" Seria asked.

Arachton regarded Seria for a while longer as she tried to suppress the need to shudder. Then Arachton started sputtering, her fangs snapping against one another as the fur on her legs rattled and hissed in movement.

After Arachton stopped, Seria stood looking at her, bewildered. "So, Arachton it is then."

"Heh," Arachton huffed, "maybe I won't have to eat this one." She turned and scurried across the floor and up the wall into the dark heights of the ceiling.

"This one really can stand her own." The hulking, yellow-scaled creature lumbered up to Seria and held out a big palm for her to shake. "I'm Harahn," he said, and at her expression he quickly added, "I'm an orc."

Seria took his hand gingerly. "What is an orc?"

"Hah!" The squat one bubbled up to her. "Your world has only humans and nymphs, yeah?"

"Yeah?"

"Well, there are a lot of worlds out there, many with only one or two races. I'm a dwarf! The name is Leppin." The dwarf took her hand from Harahn's and shook vigorously, nearly pulling her down off her feet. "You're in for a world of bizarreness. Took me a while to get used to it. The lizard-looking thing over there is from a race called Scein. His name is Drawg." Drawg nodded his greeting to Seria but kept his distance. "And you already know Rafek and Drade. Rafek's people call themselves Chimpmen, and Drade is a human, as you can see."

"I see. And Rorc?"

Leppin's face fell. "His people call themselves Felisin."

"And that's all that's left of Pride Squadron," Rafek said. "Every squadron has its own Star Fort with its own name, and they report to their own knight captain, who then reports to a knight commander, who reports to the knight general. Right now they are in a meeting, so Drade . . ." He turned to his human companion, who was moving up to one of the portals. He grunted as he hefted his captain's large body. But he bore the pain without complaint. ". . . You can break the news to them all at once."

"That would be helpful." Drade held his palm up to the inert doorway and concentrated. A moment later the empty space winked with white light and pulsed. "Except many of the commanders are assholes."

"Do you think you'll be the new knight captain?" Leppin asked, more seriously this time.

"I'd rather not, but that's up to Boln."

"You don't have to be alone when you tell him," Rafek said, stepping forward.

"Boln and Rorc recruited me, Rafek. Out of everyone here I know them the most. I should be the one to tell Boln his brother died." Drade hefted the mighty war hammer that was laid across Rorc's chest and tossed it to Rafek. "He would have wanted you to have it." Then Drade turned from them and stepped through the portal's light. He disappeared as the portal winked out of existence.

"Right." Rafek turned to Seria after a short silence, holding the enormous war hammer in both hands with reverence. "First things first, we eat. Then I show you around, and tomorrow, we train!"

Across the Cosmos . . .

The Star Citadel was the seat of power for the Knights Cosmic, a cathedral fortress of blue-hued granite that drifted through the stellar dusts and motes of celestial warmth. It was a beacon of strength for all squadrons scattered throughout the cosmos that fought existential terrors by the day. Its high towers and vast courtyards whose fountains spilled into the void were designed to reflect the eternal nature of time and life.

As mighty and large a structure as it was, it was all but unoccupied. Incurred losses were adding up. The Voir were swarming between the stars in numbers not seen since the old days—back when the stars were young and the first wisps of sentient life crawled from the mud of their respective worlds. That was a dangerous time, the first time the Voir could actually feed on something substantial in this universe. It was when the Knights Cosmic were first founded by the Sun Guardians.

Now something was stirring the Voir into a frenzy, and the council members met to discuss their response.

The Knights Council stood within their meeting chamber, a vast monument to infinity carved from a single block of stone. Golden statues of the Sun Guardians stood resolute, lining either side of the room and towering over the mortals below. The statues doubled as mighty pillars in the hallowed space, interspaced by high-arched windows which looked out across the shifting starlit tapestry. Some windows showed the deep black, others an array of starlight, wisps of celestial debris, or the worlds that circled their luminous suns.

Each arch window was framed by a portal and had a staircase leading down into the room. Running down the centre of the council space from the large doors to the balcony was a stone table, also carved from the same block of granite as the chamber. It served as a long basin, with a stream of water running through it before spilling into a fountain on the balcony and dispersing into the night. The water running through the table had magical properties, mingling with the Citadel's granite to forge a starlit map of translucent images. It was an impression of the cosmos, the territory the Knights Cosmic presided over.

Convened around the table were four humanoid knights: three were commanders, and one was the knight general of the Order. They were distinguished from other Knights Cosmic only by the crests on their helmets and the adornments on their cuirasses and pauldrons.

"Voir assaults are becoming more frequent and more deadly than ever before," the lion-maned knight said, his helm resting upon the table's rim. "I have the Roaming Wall dashing all over the cosmos, usually arriving too late to save the innocents."

"Boln," said the knight general, an elf who furrowed his rosy pink brow as he talked, "all of my commanders are reporting similar things. What would you have us do?"

"Assemble the Knights Cosmic en masse."

One of the commanders scoffed, a human woman with short dark hair and pointed features. "A mustering call to go after lone Voir one at a time? It's a waste of resources."

"Quite the opposite, Shrath," Boln growled. "I want us to gather where no Voir have been sighted, over the world Trist."

"Hah!" The other knight commander slammed his fist on the table, an aging orc whose scaled skin was turning from yellow to green, yet he still reeked of vitality. "Now that is something I had not considered. The Voir are out in force, coordinating like the mindless soul feeders they are in order to misdirect our forces!"

Shrath and the knight general chuckled along with the orc.

"Gruhtal makes a compelling point, Boln," the knight general said. "You have too keen a mind for strategy, I think. It aids you well in battle but poorly in the space between each bout. Maybe that is why your only remaining squadron still suffers dwindling numbers."

Boln resisted the urge to bare his teeth. "Please, General, I send my knights to do their job no matter the cost. And right now that means we need to realise we are being divided between worlds in a way that has never happened before. Someone is making moves against us."

"Well, you . . ." Shrath's reply was cut short when the portal behind Boln winked into existence. Drade stalked through the magical conduit into the council chamber, without his armour, and carrying the body of Rorc. "By the stars . . ."

"Sir Drade?" Boln turned, his eyes flicking between his knight and the body of his brother. "What is this? Put him on the table!" Boln rushed to grab the body from Drade, who shook his head with solemn eyes.

"It's too late for that. I regret to inform you, Boln, that your brother is dead."

"That can't be," the orc commander huffed. "As a Knight Cosmic his soul would have acquiesced with his armour and body. There would be nothing left of him once the Sun Guardians escorted him personally to his world's star."

"He was skewered in three places by the limbs of a large Voir, Commander. I tried to shield him but proved too weak. I am truly sorry, but Rorc is fallen, and some foul magic has prevented his final honour."

Boln caressed the dead face of his brother, taking the body gently in his arms and laying him on the ornate table, half submerging him in the running waters. He looked up to Shrath, who watched on with a chilled expression; he glanced at Gruhtal, then to the general. "Now do you see? There is more afoot here than the rampant attacks of mindless beasts."

"Knight . . . Sir Drade was it?" the general asked.

Drade straightened and nodded. "Yes, General."

"What can you tell us about this Voir?"

"It was different. We had it on the back foot, and then it somehow summoned more souls into its manifested body. It grew stronger, larger, more ferocious, yet it fed on no physical bodies. It almost looked like necromancy, but the Voir can't wield such a power."

"That's not possible!" Shrath interjected. "Once a Voir ingests enough souls to become manifest, it can't consume the immaterial anymore. It must seek souls sheltered within bodies."

"I am well aware, Commander," Drade said stoically. "I have been fighting this war longer than you."

"What did you say? You little . . ."

"Enough!" The general cut her short and she stifled her tirade. "You are the human knight who has refused promotions since you joined?" he asked Drade.

"Yes, General."

"Why?"

"I want to fight on the front lines. I have ever since my training was complete. And I'm telling you, this Voir was different."

"Now do you see?" Boln said. "We must muster the knights!"

The general bit his lip, considering the star map projecting from the table in ethereal brilliance, disturbed by the flow of water around Rorc's body. Points of red light on the mapped stars marked recent attacks; there were fewer near Trist than the rest of the cosmos. "I need time to consider this. By gathering our forces we leave many bereft souls unprotected."

"Decide quickly, General," Boln said. "One of those souls may be my brother's if he was not escorted to safety." He turned to Drade, walking him back to the portal with his arm around his shoulder. "Did he die well?"

"He fought with a lion's heart, sir." Drade smirked, huffing a bittersweet laugh. "I am sorry I could not save him."

"By the sounds of it, you did more than I would have asked of any of my knights." Boln looked at Drade's shoulder, which was slowly healing with glittering polyps of magic; his simple tunic was soaked in dried blood. "I suspect you would have let it pierce your heart if it came to it."

"Still, Commander, it was not enough."

"Don't do that, Drade. It wasn't your fault. You have to let go of that story in your head from . . . well, from before I found you."

"I'll work on it."

"Now, I need a new captain." Boln squeezed Drade's good shoulder.

"Rafek seems a fine choice." Drade knew it was a weak attempt.

"Aye, he is a good leader, cares for his own. But when he gets riled up, his ego takes over. I need someone who can discard his ego when the time calls for it, someone who can care for his squadron like a father would, someone who can brighten the mood when necessary or discipline with a firm, fair hand when it is required. Does that sound like anyone on the squadron to you?"

Drade considered for a moment. "Leppin?"

Boln sighed. "That dwarf can't be serious long enough to make breakfast! You know I meant you."

"Commander, I don't want to lead."

"Did you want to be a Knight Cosmic? Or was it just a necessary duty at the time?" Drade didn't answer. "Good lad, Captain Drade. Return to the Roaming Wall and ready the squadron. Orders shall be following soon."

"Yes, Commander. I should let you know we also picked up a new recruit, a water nymph named Seria."

"Train her well then. I wager we will have a fight on our hands soon enough."

"It will be done." The portal winked with white magic, and Drade made to step through.

"And, Drade." Boln spoke more softly. "Don't blame yourself for my brother's death. I know you; you've been the same ever since we found you. His death is on the Voir that killed him, not on you."

Drade stopped short, looking into the crackling bright light of the portal. "I will do my best, Boln." He stepped through, and the portal winked out of existence.

"Now, how to best recall our engaged squads?" the orc commander hummed.

The portal behind Boln flickered open again, and he turned with a perplexed expression, expecting Drade. Instead, something else stepped through and into the council room.

It was a tall creature—taller than even Boln—and was draped in a strange cloak that covered it from its shoulders to its feet. The cloak hissed against the stone floor as it dragged in the wake of the creature's steady gait. Its face was garish and stone-like, with bat ears, a snubbed pig-like nose, and a maw of fangs that grinned at the perplexed knights.

"Greetings, Knights Council," it said with a deep, rumbling voice as it stalked down the steps to the council table.

The knights growled and drew their silver, star-forged weapons on the thing.

"This is the sanctum of the Knights Cosmic. What business do you have here?" the knight general demanded.

The creature chuckled, a sound like rocks trembling against each other. It pulled a long, decrepit hand from its leathery cloak, pointing a black-taloned finger at the knights. "I am

Vurrel Maym, formerly of the Gargoyle Court, and I bring tidings to you, guardians of souls, from my master."

"Who is your master, and what tidings do they bring?" Boln growled. The flickering of the still opened portal broke his focus for an instant. *Something's not right.* As he glared back at the gargoyle, he noticed out of the corner of his eye that Shrath was inching closer towards her portal.

"Oh, Commander Boln, my master transcends even my understanding. It hails from the space between spaces and moves with a purpose that even your Sun Guardians would pale to consider." The gargoyle let his cloak splay open, revealing that it was not a cloak at all, but great bat-like wings. He drew forth a gnarled staff with a red gem set into its top and incanted a spell that blasted the knights back as sickening tendrils slithered through the portal behind him. "And the tidings are such!" his voice boomed. "You are but a steppingstone towards its goal. Your souls shall feed the great beast that musters in the dark, and the pillars of creation you fight to protect shall be shaken!" Vurrel leaped to strike at the general as the tendrils engaged the orc and Boln.

Boln fought valiantly against the onslaught. The tendrils were the ends of the twisted limbs of dozens of Voir that now poured through the portal. "Shrath!" Boln cried. "Destroy the portal! Cut them off!"

But she had already fled, opening her own portal, which led to her Star Fort. This only allowed the teaming Voir to pour through after her and wreak havoc on her fort from within.

Vurrel slammed the knight general upon the table, cracking it open, which caused some of the flowing waters to spill over the floor. The gargoyle then drove his staff through the general's chest plate, breaking through the armour and pulverising his heart. The orc was overwhelmed by even more Voir that poured through the portal, and he was quickly torn to pieces.

But Boln surged through the losing brawl with a lion's roar and made for the portal. He smashed the supporting pillars with his axe. The portal flickered out of existence, leaving only the view of the eternal night sky beyond it. A Voir that was half emerged dissolved with pained screams, and Boln turned to face the rest of his enemy.

The gargoyle weaved more magic and—to Boln's horror—all of the portals lining the chamber flickered and opened. The remaining Voir sped through them to their respective Star Forts. The Knights Cosmic would be overwhelmed from within their very fortresses. Boln smiled with grim relief, knowing that the portal to his own fort now lay in ruins behind him, knowing that Drade and his squadron were still safe.

"Who let you in here, gargoyle?" Boln bellowed as the room emptied of all but Vurrel and himself. "Who is in line to taste my axe after you?"

"Oh, Sir Boln." Vurrel chuckled and whirled his staff. The bodies of the orc and elf writhed as their souls were siphoned in green wisps into the heights of the dark ceiling. "There is so much you don't know."

An insidious slithering echoed throughout the chamber, and the souls of Boln's comrades were absorbed by an unseen creature that now pulsed and broke into corporeal form. It was a Voir of epic proportions. It shimmered, winking into existence as it fed on the fresh souls of two great Knights

Cosmic. With a terrible screech it launched itself from the heights and slammed into the lion knight.

Part II: The Prismatic Fire

Wundan didn't stop to catch his breath, didn't stop to look behind him. The carrite crashing through the undergrowth in his wake sounded close enough that he couldn't spare the time to glance. The other carrites slithered through the brush on either side of the mad-dash pursuit, keen not to intervene as it seemed they were moving towards the same destination anyway—the village that was currently being raided—Wundan's home.

Wundan slid under a log and drew his knife as the carrite dove over it. It was sleek and lean like a coyote, but had hideous, saggy black skin and a red, hooked beak for tearing through carrion. It slashed down at Wundan with its claws, and he slashed back with his knife, slicing it across the face.

The beast clucked and howled and tore away through the undergrowth. The other carrites cooed in laughter at their overzealous companion's failure. Wundan gasped and sped ahead of them, his gait faltering as the slope levelled out on the last leg towards his village.

Even from this distance, the screams were palpable. They competed to be heard over the clash of weapons and the sickening thud of metal impacting flesh and bone.

He was too late. The raiders were inside.

A group of villagers fled through the gates only to be shot or ridden down by horsemen with nets and spears. Some were being rounded up . . . and that meant Wundan's mum might still be alive . . .

"I have to get to her."

Wundan ignored the incessant clicking of the approaching carrites, ignored the bile in his throat, and he tore through the patches of wooded farms towards the smell of smoke and burning flesh.

Twenty years later

Despite countless myths that stated otherwise, nymphs could bleed. Of course they could; they just had to be distracted enough that they couldn't turn into a water form around the blade that bled them. That's what Seria was so pissed off about when the iron tang of her own blood oozed over her tongue. She was pissed not that she had been struck, but that she had lost focus.

She didn't have time to regain her focus because Rafek's body slammed her into the training floor. The top-heavy weight of the monkey-like thing knocked the wind out of her.

"Again," Drade said, oblivious to her winded grunt, "and this time try not to fail so much."

Seria spat the blue fluid from her mouth as Rafek chuckled and rolled off her. Drade had been different since he came back through the portal from the Knights Council. He wasn't monotone and dutiful; instead—without his armour conjured—he was sassy and upbeat, and it egged Rafek on insufferably.

"Yeah, ook ook!" Rafek chortled, a laugh that rolled up from his belly. "A Voir would have had time to dissect you before you summoned your armour."

"Look!" Seria barked as she struggled up. "I don't KNOW how to summon this fucking armour! You say you can *sense* the Celestial Spark or some bullshit, but maybe you just saw a lonesome nymph in the wild and decided you needed a new servant to dust this fucking castle!"

Leppin chuckled and looked around. "The place could use a dusting actually."

The training arena was the cleanest room in the Roaming Wall by far, and that was purely because it received the most use from the squadron. The dust simply didn't have enough time to settle before it was disturbed by the constant ruckus the knights caused.

Arachton scuttled somewhere in the high rafters, and a dust trail fell behind her. "I don't mind. It makes a nice place to find bugs," she said.

"Well, maybe you should stop focusing on those bugs and feast on the rats that got into the pantry like you said you would!" Rafek barked up to her.

"Why would I feed on the rats *before* they are fattened?" Arachton retorted. She swung down by a web that spooled from her abdomen and landed on the side of the arena where Drade was smirking.

"It defeats the point of you telling us not to worry about them!" Drade said, shoving her playfully. "It's no good to us if you kill them *after* they've eaten through the food."

"EXCUSE ME!" Seria yelled, marching right up to Drade. A fire was burning deep within her, so hot that water steamed from her pores. "How does this nonsense help me channel my fire?"

The squadron stifled as Drade stared her down. All of a sudden her fire petered out and her steaming ceased.

"Do you feel . . ." Drade spoke in that monotone now, his soft features hardening without so much as a flicker of movement, ". . . hard done by?"

Seria willed her voice not to squeak. "Yes."

Drade's stern stare cracked. "Excellent! Hold onto that feeling!" He clapped her on the shoulder with a beaming smile and marched into the arena. "Now, a paladin's power is bestowed upon them by the Sun Guardians. This is for their service to the divine . . . or purity or peace or . . . whatever it is paladins tell themselves." Drade waved his hands in a dismissive manner. "But a Knight Cosmic's power is something inherent in us from birth. It emerges in response to a need, specifically a need to rectify a wrong. The Voir feed on lost souls, people who find themselves adrift in the void through no fault of their own. This is usually a fate reserved for the wretched. The wretched are so few, they aren't enough to sustain a Voir until it becomes corporeal. But as you have seen, things often go wrong. Many good souls are consumed." Drade sighed before continuing. "When this wrong—when a Voir—is presented to someone with the Celestial Spark, it can ignite. This conjures Prismatic Fire, which forms our armour, grants us power, and allows us to soar between the stars. It might manifest in the uninitiated as anger, but the real word for it is fury. A righteous rage bent to righting a wrong. This is the power one gains when evil rears its head and must be smote."

"I prefer to say smitten, ook, ook." Rafek laughed.

"Shut it," Drade said seriously, then turned back to Seria. "Did that Voir in the swamps attack anyone close to you?"

"No, it . . ." She paused, biting back the rising fire.

"Don't resist it," Drade said, and beckoned for her to continue.

"It barrelled down on an old human lady. Frail . . . she couldn't move fast enough. The scream was . . ."

"And so you acted." Drade's skin was pulsing. "With that feeling, and the Spark, you can conjure *vast* power." Drade shone brighter and his armour coalesced; it had changed since he went through the portal, promoted now to knight captain. His helm had a crest that fanned backwards, and his pauldrons and chest plate had similar decorations.

"So when Rafek was pummelling me just now, it was to help me feel that feeling?" Seria asked, squinting through Drade's light.

"No," Drade said. His armour faded and his warm demeanour returned somewhat. "Rafek is just an asshole. Now focus on that feeling, remember the old woman, remember the sound she made when the Voir got her."

Seria gasped and the heat within her flared.

"You weren't capable of saving her." Drade's words bit like cold steel. "Focus on what you would have needed to help her—armour, strength, speed; you had none of it. You couldn't do *anything* . . ."

Seria started panting. Her eyes scrunched closed, her brow furrowed, and steam billowed from her skin.

"Channel the feeling, channel the *need*."

Seria cried out and her skin shimmered for a moment before the light winked out of existence, and then she collapsed on the ground sobbing.

"It's okay, little one." Drade leaned down and clasped his strong hand over her shoulder. "That was brilliant."

"But it wasn't!" she cried. "I couldn't save that woman!"

"You can save the next one. Remember, focus on the need."

Coarse, grating rage ebbed from Seria's innards, replaced by the smooth flow of the cool, calm waters that she imagined her emotions to be. Drade spoke to her like something she could not quite describe. He was a vast ocean, with darkness and crushing depths the further into him you looked. But he was also pristine, fresh and full of life and movement about the surface. She looked up into his deep, dark eyes and nodded.

"Need," she said. "How will I know I'm ready?"

"Because you'll have to be," Drade responded.

"Map room's blinking." Drawg—the lizard man—scurried into the training arena, breaking their moment.

Seria coughed and righted herself as she realised the others were all watching her training intently. "Map room?" she asked.

Drade chuckled, but then his eyes turned hard again. "Knights, map room, now."

The Squadron picked themselves up and bumbled out of the training arena like a pack of hooligans let loose from class—loud and boisterous. They ushered into a compact room by the common nexus. The room was carved from starlit stone with a trough leading from the wall to a floating basin in the centre . . .

No, Seria realised. *It is not a trough. It's a low-lying aqueduct.* The knights piled in around the basin that the aqueduct fed.

"Lights," Drade ordered.

Rafek clambered around the room and smothered the torchlight in the small space. As their flames winked out, a luminescent blue light emanated from the stone that made up the room, particularly from the stone in the well of the basin.

"Water," Drade ordered.

Leppin huffed and jumped up to the sluice lever where the aqueduct protruded from the wall. He grabbed the lever—or more accurately, hung from it—pulling it down with his weight, raising the sluice gate. The familiar bubbling of flowing water poured down the aqueduct and into the basin, circling around it before siphoning out through a drain in the bottom.

As the waters flowed through the basin, something wonderful happened.

Seria gasped as her eyes filled with stars.

From the depths of the stone basin, thousands, *millions* of bright lights sprang into the room along with nebulous dust clouds.

"What in the . . ." Seria reached out to one of the stars in wonder and giggled in delight as it splashed and rippled at her touch before returning to normal.

"From here, Seria, the Knights Cosmic can coordinate," Drade said. "There is very powerful magic that conjures when the stone meets with water, which shows us the movement of lost souls in the ether. They're shown as green. This room also warns us of Voir energy spikes. This happens when they are about to become corporeal and feast on the living."

"Those are the orange, throbbing lights." Rafek grunted and pointed to one.

"And the blue lights are other Star Forts like the Roaming Wall." Arachton pointed to several of them with her many legs.

"What is this spot?" Seria pointed to a star that had no visible movement of knights, Voir, or souls.

"Ah, that is Trist, a world where most species of the cosmos live," Rafek said. "It was founded many millennia ago by travellers between the worlds who used magic. There were many wars, many species did not like each other, but certain members of their races enjoyed the variety. Most of those travellers are now dead, and Trist, like other worlds, lives in isolation from the others. Many who know of it are surprised it still lives."

"But there is nothing happening there?" Seria asked. *Not even soul movements . . .* Every world had a stream of green channelling into their suns, but not Trist.

"No," Drade answered, "but there is a shitload happening elsewhere. Look at this, guys. Star Forts are heading in all different directions chasing more and more Voir incidents."

"Things are getting out of hand," Harahn tutted.

"Especially here at Aefellion," Arachton hissed and pointed to an orange and blue convergence. "A whole Star Fort at an Arachtoid world, and the Voir glow persists. It isn't far, Drade. We should lend assistance."

"But there is a Voir attack brewing here, a star over. We should not leave it abandoned," Rafek said, "especially as the Arachtoids already have a Knights Cosmic presence."

Drade studied the worlds thoughtfully. "That's Hord Squadron . . . They have more knights than any other squadron.

If they are bogged down, the Voir there must be formidable . . . but Rafek is right. It would leave this region undefended. I'm not sure what we should do."

"Come on, Drade, leave the Arachtoids with Hord Squadron," Rafek suggested with a cheeky grin. "It's not like people enjoy having an Arachtoid colony this close to their home world anyway. Let them fend for themselves lest they survive to send forth another warpath."

"And how many war bands have your monkey kind sent out in search of fucking fruits?" Arachton's hairs bristled, causing Seria to shiver.

"A fair point." Rafek puffed his chest. "I only jest, noble critter."

"Rafek, Arachton," Drade said, ignoring their squabble. "I need you both to head through the portal to Hord Squadron's Fort. Then report back to me. I am going to direct the Roaming Wall to this Voir presence nearby. It's only a small incursion, great practice for our new recruit."

"If you insist, Captain. Ook, ook, you are so bossy since you got a crest on your helmet!"

"Don't give me that shit, Rafek. Just get it done."

Leppin ceased the water flow, and the star map faded from view as the waters that fed the basin drained. The knights shuffled out into the common nexus, and Rafek and Arachton headed for one of the inert portals.

"So, how do you steer the Roaming Wall?" Seria asked.

"It responded to my decision the moment I made it. Its magic and mine are linked," Drade answered.

"I see."

"Then explain why this blasted portal won't open!" Rafek yelled from the inert portal.

Drade furrowed his brow and stalked up to it, staring it down with smouldering intensity. "What the fuck is happening?" he muttered. "Leppin, Drawg, Harahn, check the other portals."

The knights bustled around the different portals and stood by them, frowning when none winked into existence.

"None are working, boss. We are cut off from the other Star Forts," Harahn said.

"Could Rorc's death have affected the Roaming Wall?" Arachton asked.

"It did, until his brother made the puny human here the new captain," Harahn said.

"Please, shut up." Drade paced the nexus, going from portal to portal. "Whatever has happened, it doesn't change the immediate threat. Rafek, Arachton, get to Hord Squadron."

"It'll take days to go via pillars of fire!" Rafek said.

"Then you better get gone, now," Drade replied. "Something is amiss. Be careful and report back as soon as you are able."

"Yes, Cap'n!" Rafek saluted as he and Arachton summoned their armour and flew out of the doors of the nexus towards the gate. Jets of Prismatic Fire pirouetted in their wake.

"But that leaves us so few?" Sierra asked.

"No matter, liquid one," Drawg said. "Five Knights Cosmic can face down any threat in the cosmos."

"That seems a dubious boast," Seria said, "but I'm sure we'll soon find out."

The Roaming Wall drifted through the tendril wisps of stellar debris, and Pride Squadron—minus Rafek and Arachton—stood at the gate in their translucent, technicoloured armour.

"Guardians help us," Leppin breathed.

Drade was silent, staring down the scene with a brimming fury that threatened to boil over.

"What?" Seria looked into the black void bordered by stars eons in the other direction. She was the only one among them who was unarmoured. "I see nothing."

"Focus your fire," Drade all but spat.

His voice was hard again while he channelled his righteous fury. His armour grew denser as he spoke, pulsed brighter as he breathed.

Seria did as she was told and focused back on that need, standing only in her robes on the precipice of the abyss. Images flickered before her eyes of great Voir monstrosities and terrified, disembodied faces. Their screams echoed on non-existent winds. The sound rose and died in her heart as her concentration broke.

"What was that?" she gasped.

"Focus!" Drade ordered.

Seria focused her need, and the ethereal images re-faded into existence before her. Voir in their dozens were feasting on fleeing souls in the abyss, growing larger and more corporeal with every victim.

"How, how can we fight them when they aren't corporeal yet?"

"Our weapons from the armoury give us that privilege," Harahn answered. "The silver is forged in the hearts of the stars. They themselves are ethereal by nature."

"But I have none." Seria's shoulders drooped. She was helpless to do anything to help the poor souls who were being slaughtered before her very eyes. "I can do nothing."

"And you will do nothing but guard the Roaming Wall," Drade ordered. "You are not ready for this contest, water nymph. Harahn, throw open the soul gate, and let them take refuge while we fell these beasts."

Harahn grunted and threw his hand out. Gates on the outer walls opened in response to his call. The souls—green wisps of now dead people—poured into the safety of the Fort, pooling in the common nexus behind the knights.

"Once we have secured these souls," Harahn explained to Seria, who looked back at the nexus in wonder, "we can escort them safely to their stars for the afterlife. You stay here, little one. Let us do battle with these fiends."

"Knights!" Drade barked, and the four knights launched out of the Roaming Wall on jets of fire to clash with the Voir.

All Seria could do was watch as they battled. The Voir looked like decomposing maggots—like the one she had already battled on her home world. Yet these were still ghostly things at this stage of their development. They had large, nightmarish mouths at their heads, with rows upon rows of teeth lining the whole throat down to their innards. And they had dozens of horrible spidery legs sprouting irregularly out of their grey, gelatinous flesh all the way up and down their segmented bodies.

They screeched like scraping metal and met the knights in combat.

Seria watched in wonder—and then in horror—as one of the Voir slipped past the knights' formation. It tore through the ether towards the Roaming Wall—open and unguarded, save for Seria . . .

"Drade!" she cried into the embroiled abyss, "Captain Drade!" but her voice could not carry over the air that was not there, over the void between the Roaming Wall and the magically sealed atmosphere around the knights' armour. She could not warn them unless she, too, conjured her armour.

The ethereal Voir ripped a swathe through a stream of souls, scooping them up in its horrid jaws and munching down as their unearthly wails reached Seria's ears. She was transported back to Marsil, where that frail old woman was trying to hobble out of the beast's path.

But Seria *still* couldn't do anything.

Drade, Leppin, Drawg, and Harahn dispatched a lesser Voir and converged on the largest one on the far side of the fray, driving it further into the abyss with lance and sword and fire. The Voir threatening the Roaming Wall had nothing to stop it as it crashed straight through the gates—passing through Seria like a ghost—and consuming the souls in the nexus at its leisure. With each kill it grew larger, more corporeal, relishing in the suffering of its victims. It keened and vibrated in apparent ecstasy as it bound their energy—their essence—into its insidious flesh.

Seria scrunched her eyes and focused on the Fire that sparked deep within her. This was not her simmering water, not her churning seas, nor frothing madness—this was *Fire*. It raged and spread throughout her, burning all that it touched. With a flash of colour she wrenched her eyes open and focused on her target—the Voir—that had just now noticed her.

Her hair ruffled and her robes billowed in the windless void. She screamed as the fire burst forth from her, enveloped her, and formed protective translucent plate armour.

She had conjured her Prismatic Fire. And the Voir reared in fear as it recognised her for what she was, a threat.

Her helm formed last, the faceplate slamming over her snarling visage. "Get your fucking maw away from these people!" Seria screamed.

She lurched forward—not caring that she had no weapon—and slammed into the Voir with speed she had never known, with strength she could never hope to possess, and with a rage . . . It was a rage she hoped never to stifle.

She slammed into the beast and knocked it back into the walls of the common nexus. It screeched pathetically, a coward caught in the act of bullying. And it was a coward in the truest sense of the word. It had not expected resistance; it had sniffed out the weak and the helpless, and for that Seria was going to make it *pay*.

It slammed her with its tail. It had not yet taken physical form, but as Seria had summoned her armour, she now contended with it in its realm. She flew back from the impact and smashed into the far table. Coughing, she leaped up on a pillar of fire and urged the souls to shy back and keep their distance.

The green, ephemeral wisps obeyed her urge.

She reached forth her hand, feeling something call to her from the armoury. *Her* weapon—a great halberd of star-forged silver—burst through the astral doors it was housed behind. It raced towards her grasp and fit into her hand like one would fit into the embrace of an old lover. The halberd—the star spear—had chosen her, and she had accepted it.

Seria lowered her new weapon to menace the Voir as it tried to twist away and flee. It was fast, but it only had one exit, and she knew where to strike. She aimed for the gates and jetted towards them on pillars of flame. She reached the gates when the Voir did and skewered it through and through—a death blow. It cried and writhed and burned and shrivelled into nothing.

Seria hefted her halberd and roared in fury, "You shan't harm another soul!"

She heaved, unable to contain the brimming emotions. Her armour was a paradox. It warmed her like a mug of tea between her palms on a cold day, and it burned like a hot bath at the same time. It hurt in a comforting way, like tearing off an old scab. It was a release, an easing of tension to finally wear her flame, her fury, her Fire. But the pain was becoming too much.

She gazed at the other knights and called to them. They had driven the Voir into oblivion and were soaring back to her. She expected cheers, congratulations . . . but when they landed, as their helmets dissolved from their faces and they entered the Roaming Wall, their expressions were that of fear.

Drade's was that of fury.

"W-what's wrong?" Seria asked as her armour dissipated.

"Incorporeal Voir are unable to enter a Star Fort," Leppin said.

Drade clenched his fists so tight that his star-forged sword quivered in his grip. "Something is terribly wrong . . ."

Part III: Scattered Lights

As he got closer to the burning town, little Wundan ducked to the side of the forested road and scurried into the foliage. The carrites didn't have the gall to swoop in this close while conflict still raged; he was safe . . . from them.

Another group of villagers burst through the gates. Before they could make it twenty paces, a hidden group of bandits sprung a trap from either side of the road. The slaughter was quick and horrific.

Petrified, Wundan froze mid-crawl. He was not more than an arm's length away from where the nearest bandit leaped out from a brush.

His heart was in his throat, and he forced himself to hold his breath lest they heard him. His panic rose with the thrumming in his ears, drumming harder with each passing second.

His eyes flitted over the corpses, trying to see if his mother was among them through the tears that poured freely down his face.

No, none were of his mother, but he recognised the shoemaker. The whites of his eyes were bloodshot and stared into the nothingness where Wundan was huddled. Then he saw the milkmaid, clutching her son to her bosom—both skewered—and then he recognised the bodies of the stable hands.

The pain of seeing friends dead and of holding all of that emotion at bay as he held his breath grew too great. His chest felt as if it might burst, so little Wundan gasped, inhaling the rancid, smoke-throttled air.

One of the bandits grunted and looked up from his looting, scanning the brush.

The bandits were all human, wearing crude leather garments and sporting cruel-looking knives or cudgels.

"What is it?" one of the bandits asked.

"I thought I heard something," the first one said.

"It's probably that pack of carrites that have been shadowing us since we started raiding."

"They'll find more use off these poor bastards than we will," another of the bandits said as he kicked the shoemaker, rolling his body over to rifle through his pockets. "I mean, fuck, do these peasants have anything of value?"

"Mull made it clear when we signed up. We attack the small towns to build up for the big one. There is an orc village next—they'll be a little tougher than this lot. Then we reach a multispecies settlement on the coast on the far side of the mountains. They'll have the most spoils. And we'll be ready to take it all."

"So what do we do in the meantime?"

A woman screamed within the burning village, one that rang out in greater woe than the others as the sound of conflict died down. The band of bandits looked over to the smouldering town and laughed.

"Well, like Mull said, in the meantime we enjoy a bit of sport with these worms."

The scream caught Wundan's ear too, because it was drawn from his mother. She was still alive, and these bandits were laughing at her pain. Wundan gripped his dagger in trembling hands, eyeing the open gate, taking bigger and bigger breaths as he prepared himself for what he had to do.

With a yell he charged out of the brush, reaching the bandit who heard him before and slashing at his leg.

"What the fuck!" The bandit jumped back as his leg spilled open and Wundan rushed past him, ducking around a stray arm. "That little shit just knifed me! Gut him!"

But Wundan had already scooted between them, charging towards the open gates, which were starting to catch aflame. Through the opening was a wall of thick black smoke. Wundan steeled himself and barrelled inside.

He made it past the gates, bursting through plumes of smoke and stopping to stare in horror at his pillaged town. But the blood and ruin filtered from his mind as he sighted his mother in the centre. Standing over her sprawled form was a large man. He wore a dark cloak and brandished a wickedly curved sword.

Wundan's mother tried to crawl away from him, and froze when she saw her son, standing with a feeble dagger in his hands. She cried out for him to run. But the bandits outside closed in behind him, and the one he had slashed clobbered him across the back of his head . . .

Twenty years later

"What magic could undo that of the Knights Cosmic?" Drawg hissed. "We are mandated by the divine; none can withstand our might."

"And yet," Drade said coolly, watching as Harahn ushered the souls further back into the Roaming Wall's chambers, "Captain Rorc's soul was not guided by a Sun Guardian. By all accounts, it is likely he was ingested by the corporeal Voir."

"But that CAN'T happen," Drawg said.

"ENOUGH!" Drade's voice filled the room with a flush of heat, leaving the hot metal aftertaste of Prismatic Fire. "Things that can't happen have kept on happening. Firstly, Voir aren't supposed to grow in size until *after* they've ingested enough souls to reach critical mass and pass into the physical realm. But they are, through some use of necromancy. Then Rorc's soul was not escorted to safety, and then the portals stopped working . . . and now an ephemeral Voir breaches the Roaming Wall, OUR STAR FORT!" Drade breathed deeply, his shoulders heaving. "I fear something terrible is happening, and it has been happening for a while, but we were just too fucking powerless to stop it."

Drade went to the nearest table and grabbed it with a roar. His armour flared into existence for a split second as he flipped the table against the far wall. It smashed to bits against the starlit stone, and the crockery upon it shattered.

Leppin hobbled up to him. "Drade, these events aren't a reflection of the time you were recruited."

"Are you saying that because you think I don't know?" Drade spun on the dwarf. "No, it's not like before, because this time I don't have any excuse to be letting everyone down!"

"The dwarf speaks the truth, Captain." Harahn lumbered over from the rear wall of the hall since he had finished shepherding the souls. "And you speak a perverted version of the truth."

Drade turned to the orc, his glare unwavering. "Then what should I do with Leppin's truth?"

"Let go of what has happened, Drade," Harahn said. "Lead in the now. We need your strength."

Seria tensed. It looked like Drade was about to attack Harahn, but to her amazement he took a deep breath and seemed to simmer down.

"My strength is useless if I can't direct it anywhere. And I can't go through a portal to warn the council. We need a new plan."

"We need to regroup." Seria stepped forward tentatively. "From the star map it seemed the Knights Cosmic are scattered across the cosmos. Even our own squadron is scattered, as we had to send Rafek and Arachton on a separate mission. Should we not regroup with another squadron? Or is that not how we do things?"

"We can do it; it's just that all the squadrons have friendly rivalries," Drawg hissed. "Regrouping will lead to decades of roasting at our expense."

"It's the reason Rafek and Arachton were keen to travel to help Hord Squadron," Leppin chuckled, "because they could rub it in if they needed to offer assistance."

Seria couldn't help but smile. "That is idiotic."

"I agree," Drade said. "With both your plan and your last statement. I'm directing the Roaming Wall to the nearest star to offload our souls. Once we ferry our souls into the star's protection, we will head for the closest Star Fort for assistance. Until then, Seria, you just unlocked your armour; we must train you further. Fighting a wraith Voir in single combat is a feat all on its own, but it is nothing compared to the horrors I fear we must face."

"Can we face such horrors?" Seria asked.

"Never fear, water nymph." Drawg scurried up to her, placing a scaly red arm around her shoulders. "Five Knights Cosmic can face down any threat in the cosmos."

"So you keep saying . . ."

Pillars of Prismatic Fire jetted from the legs of the two Knights Cosmic as they hurtled between the stars. Travelling long distances using the multicoloured flames is different from jumping from a planet to a Star Fort; it takes more of a toll on the mind and body.

But Rafek and Arachton were seasoned knights—even if they didn't act like it between battles—and they could handle the burden. The passing was made easier by the stellar scenery.

Rafek gazed in awe at the passing polyps of light that were celestial bodies—stars and planets and drifting tides of nebula—as they streamed through the eternal night upon lances of technicoloured light and flame. His big eyes reflected their speckled journey, even beneath his translucent faceplate.

Arachton hurtled alongside of him in his periphery. She drifted side to side, enjoying her own flight. The eight jets from each of her legs combined to form a much brighter pillar in her wake.

Eventually, the world they journeyed towards loomed into their path. It was a pale brown dot amidst the sea of celestial beauty. It grew quickly, like a stone that had been hurled at them with all the strength of the giants of old.

Rafek and Arachton reacted as one, rearing to bring their legs in front of them and stall their jettison across the stars. The world now hung before them. It was an orb of pale brown beauty with wisps of white cloud clinging to it, like liquid between the two glass layers of a marble.

"Nice planet your kind chose," Rafek grunted. "A bit brown for my liking, though."

"My kind sees more colours than you, monkey."

"So, like, different kinds of brown then? Ook ook!" Rafek laughed.

Arachton rolled several of her eyes. "Let's just find the Star Fort and see what's taking them so long. It must be orbiting the far side of the world. Let's go."

"Yeah, but I'm also wondering, where is this Voir threat?" Rafek hummed.

"We can hover here in space like limp egg sacs, or we can go ask Hord Squadron ourselves." Arachton's legs quivered.

Rafek held his hands up in a placating manner, with an involuntary "Ook ook" laugh.

The two then jettisoned off, arching around the world with streaks of aurora trailing in their wake.

"Debris," Rafek said as a hail of pebble-sized chunks dinged off his faceplate and pauldrons.

"It's the same stone as a Star Fort," Arachton hissed, "starlit granite."

"How can you tell?" Rafek wondered.

"It has a celestial taste." Arachton shrugged with two of her legs.

"You eat pieces of the Star Fort?"

"No! But much of the vermin I feed on is coated in the stuff from living in the walls." Rafek shivered at this, and Arachton scoffed back at him, "Don't give me that shit. I've seen you pick and eat from your own fur!"

"Fair enough," Rafek said. "Look, there is more up ahead."

The two soared towards a dense cluster of debris that looked more like an asteroid field.

"They were attacked," Rafek gasped. "The Star Fort I mean . . . There is a trail of debris that slams into the mountain ranges on the world below. The Fort . . . it fell."

"We need to get down there!" Arachton said. "There could be survivors, they could still be under attack . . . and the citizens are still in danger."

Rafek squinted through his visor. "What about warning Drade and the others?"

"If both of us flee to tell Drade, then the survivors may die. If one of us leaves, the one who stays will be overwhelmed. But perhaps the both of us will have a chance here, together."

"We risk much here, Arachton." Rafek hefted Rorc's war hammer, now *his* war hammer. "Know that I do not recoil from this battle out of fear or panic. If we fall, Drade is down two knights and is none the wiser to the threat."

"I understand, but surely you feel as I do?" Arachton asked.

"Yes, our fellow knights must be rescued, and the people here must be protected."

"Then we are agreed?"

"We are. Lead the way, Spider Knight."

Arachton unslung her halberd from her back, gripping it with the claws at the end of her front four legs. With a burst of power, she hurtled towards the world, arching down into the air like a burning comet and slowing as she made for the mountain range below. Rafek followed right behind her, and they trailed in the ephemeral wake of the defeated Star Fort.

They kept their fears to themselves, but they both pondered on what in the cosmos could overwhelm a Star Fort. A force of dozens of Voir could maybe defeat a full squadron of knights . . . but to bring a Star Fort crashing down from orbit . . .

They stopped burning, having broken through the atmosphere to find themselves in a dusk-lit sky. They soared over a craggy brown mountain range that was littered with detritus and chunks of starlit stone.

"Can you see any of your kind?" Rafek asked.

"None. If we can help it, we live underground. It is likely the mountains are teaming with my people. Look!" Arachton gestured forward. "Something great burns just over that ridge."

They sped over the rocky outcropping, soaring high over the scene, and balked in horror. Hord Squadron's Star Fort lay in partial ruin across the mountainside. It was cracked and crumbled almost down to a single battlement, upon which several Knights Cosmic fought valiantly against a swarm of Voir.

"I have never seen more than a handful of Voir . . ." Rafek's voice wavered before he found his resolve. "Where could they find the souls to fuel such an abominable force? Millions must have been scattered between the stars for them to be fattened so . . . But from where?"

“The knights directed the fort to crash here on purpose.” Arachton pointed with a trembling limb. “Look, they are blocking an entrance to the catacombs below the mountains.”

Rafek followed her gesture but could not see the entrance clearly. He saw only more Voir embroiled in a battle with spider things that blended in with their surrounds. A lone Knight Cosmic stood with them.

Rafek blanched. “No one would willingly crash their fort!”

“They must have been crashing anyway, and they picked the best spot. Come, you reinforce the knights on the battlement. I will help my kind at the entrance to the underworld!”

Rafek bellowed a roar that would make the beasts of the deep jungle tremble and streaked down on his Pillar of Fire. He slammed into the crenulations that were being overrun by slimy, writhing, scuttling Voir.

They were foul creatures with grotesque, bloated, maggoty bodies and irregular protruding spider limbs that snapped like dead tree branches as they moved. They embodied the disgusting ambulation of a slug with the unnatural scuttling of a spider.

As Rafek brought his mighty war hammer to bear—crushing the cylindrical snapping maw of an over eager Voir—he smiled. Arachton *hated* him for comparing their motion to a spider’s, which is why he usually did it.

“Ook ook!” Rafek laughed as he flung another beast down the mountainside with a blow from his new hammer. “Monkey Knight stronk!” He walloped another Voir, crushing its head with a shriek as it rose above its flailing comrades.

"From where do you hail, Monkey Knight?" A knight propelled herself past Rafek and skewered a Voir into the crenulations. She was an ogre, tall and burly—dwarfing Rafek by a large magnitude—and had enormous antlers protruding from her helm. She spoke with a slow, lumbering voice.

"I hail from Pride Squadron. YARGH!" Rafek walloped another Voir into the abyssal heights. "Captain Drade was concerned that the Voir warning was not snuffed out by your extended presence. He sent me and Sister Knight Arachton to find out what you're up to! Where is your captain?"

"He died when the fort impacted the mountainside. We were overwhelmed from within!"

"What?"

"The Voir tore through our own portals en masse as we prepared to face the threat here. We lost the fort within seconds. Captain Tulk used his last efforts to drop it here and seal the breach in the Arachtoid stronghold below us . . . I fear it was for nothing."

Rafek bared his fangs, even though only a hint of them was visible through his translucent helm. "I must warn my squadron."

"You'll have to survive this first!"

Down on the ruined mountainside—by the open mouth of the Arachtoid fortress—Arachton was a bastion of defence against the dozens of smaller Voir that were trying to swarm through. Behind her, her kin were spinning webs and moving debris into position to seal the breach while her fellow knights were already dead and dying. She would not be able to hold them for long.

The knight battling on her right finally succumbed to his wounds as he was pierced in several places by the dead, bark-like limbs of the Voir. His corpse was tossed back into the swarm to be torn to shreds, for his armour to be broken, and for his soul to be devoured in insult to the contract between the Knights Cosmic and the Sun Guardians.

Arachton hissed in fury, and her kin hissed in response.

"Rafek!" she cried up the battlement. "We are being overwhelmed! Retreat below ground!"

Rafek heard his comrade's call and spread word among the dwindling knights on the battlement. As they fell back from the crenulations, they ignited their pillars of Prismatic Fire and propelled themselves from danger, arching down to the narrowing breach in the underground Arachtoid fortress.

Arachton held the tide back with desperate fury until most of the knights were through, and until her kind had retreated into the dark. A light flashed and a knight landed behind her. It was Rafek.

He grabbed her by the collar of her armour and hauled her through the gap as the final member of her kind pulled boulders down into place with its webs. The rumbling, cascading stones clouded the cave in darkness before the dancing, coloured light from the knights' armour lit the room. The screeching Voir outside raked at the mountainside, trying to claw their way in through the hard stone where the Arachtoids had made their home. The breathless panting of the knights and civilians within the hold were the only counter to the horrible noise outside.

"All right," Rafek grunted, startling the spiderlings around them. "They won't be held back for long . . . We need to defeat our enemy, protect these people, and warn all of the Knights Cosmic of the threat."

"But how?" The ogre was on her backside, slumped against the wall. The shimmer from her armour faded with her fury until she wore nothing but drab cloth. "How can we come back from this defeat?"

"This is not a defeat," Arachton said. "Whenever our late captain experienced a setback, he would call it a consolidation. We must take time to regroup, to think and to plan."

There was a titanic screech from without; the walls rumbled, and dust fell from the cave's ceiling.

"Well then." Another of the knights—a centaur—stood. "Let's get to work."

Part IV: The Citadel of Stars

Dark, throbbing pulses threatened to burst Wundan's head wide open. The next thing he noticed was the smell of burned flesh, shit, and smoke, and then the sounds tumbled into his awareness. They were lowly groans of people left for dead, the weeping of those few remaining, the roar of fire . . . and laughter.

Wundan gritted his teeth and forced himself to open his eyes. Even muted by thick smoke, the daylight pierced into him like a lance of pain. He winced, shutting his eyes and burying his face into the damp earth, but he tried to get up regardless.

"Oh hey there, lookee here, lads, the one with spirit has got a bit of nerve to back him up. Help him up!"

Powerful hands grabbed Wundan by the cuff and hauled him to his feet. The throbbing intensified and threatened to knock him back down, but the hands held him in place even as he retched.

"Yeah, my lad was a bit heavy-handed with you, I'll give you that." Even with blurred vision, Wundan could tell the man—Mull, the bandit leader—was sneering by the sound of his voice. "It's good for a young man like you. Hardens you up to the world. If you survive long enough, that is."

The bandits laughed in echo to his.

"Mum." Wundan's voice was a wavering weed in the breeze, quickly stomped out by passersby.

"Aw, boys," one of the men holding him taunted, "he's calling for his mummy."

"Ah, that's sweet, that's really sweet. Do you think she's still alive?" Mull said.

"That bitch on the pyre sure screamed something fierce when we hit him."

Pyre? Wundan's mind raced. *A funeral pyre? But she was still alive . . . oh gods.* The grief threatened to spill from him like a breaking dam. *I was too late.*

"Well, wake her up then. Let's see if she's his mumma!"

The dam receded, hope shoring up the cracks in his psyche.

A ringing of metal caused Wundan to jerk up and face the bandit leader as he stalked over to him, knife in hand. He held the tip of the blade to Wundan's chin, forcing him to look up into the dark, terrible eyes of his taunting captor.

"If she is your mother, little whelp, then you should feel relieved. I'll let her live, if you do one thing for me first."

Twenty years later

Seria sat silently, and Drade stared at the inert portal, motionless. He was still wearing his armour, which pulsed and sparked as the translucent colours cascaded down the ethereal plate like a waterfall. It was mesmerising, and the only sign—to Seria at least—that he was still alive.

It was also terrifying.

The sheer fury she had to wield to keep her armour for only a short while was almost too much to bear . . . and he was just . . . standing there, brimming with torrents of rage without so much as a twitch of muscle.

"How long has he been standing there do you think?" Leppin whispered to her, stroking his long beard.

Leppin, Harahn, and Drawg had done a sweep of the Roaming Wall to check for more incorporeal Voir. They had ushered the souls into safer chambers as the fort drifted towards the closest sun in order to ferry those spirits to the afterlife. The three knights had only in the last few moments returned from their duties.

"It's been half a day at least," Seria said.

"How long are days on your world?" Drawg asked as he scraped filth from his scales with a long talon.

Seria regarded him with a raised brow. "About ten hours, depending on the season."

"Hmm." Drawg licked his lips. "How long are hours on your world?"

Seria's brow furrowed. "I don't know . . . like, the regular length, I guess?"

Drawg hummed again—seemingly placated—and Seria breathed a sigh of relief.

"By the way," Harahn placed his mighty hands on her tiny shoulders, "you should be very proud of what you accomplished."

"What do you mean?" Seria suppressed a gasp; Harahn's hands were large and heavy.

"It usually takes weeks for one to summon their armour, weeks more to be ready to have star-forged silver heed their call, and you did it within days." The orc was chuffed, huffing with admiration for the water nymph.

"*And* you wielded them both in combat," Leppin added. "You're a mean knight to fuck with, no mistake."

Seria felt her cheeks grow warm. "Well, thank you."

"Not used to praise?" Drawg hissed.

"My people did not like me much, I think. They were calm waters while I was a rapid river or a crashing wave. The humans on my world called me mean-spirited, but I just didn't let them walk all over me like they did my kind."

"Heh," Harahn squeezed her shoulders, causing her to grit her teeth, "you'll fit right in with us then."

"Fellow knight." Drawg nodded.

"Fellow knight!" Leppin echoed and tapped her with his fist, his dwarf stature making the commemorative contact strike her belly.

Seria recoiled and laughed as she wriggled from Harahn's well-meaning but painful grip, and that's when Drade twitched, spinning on the spot.

Seria cut her laugh short, and the other knights straightened as Drade marched over to them.

"What's the plan, Captain?" Leppin asked.

"We're approaching the star. Something else approaches too, something big." His voice was calm and steady, but his armour flared brightly.

"How do you know?" Seria asked.

Drade jerked his finger over their shoulders to the map room; the edges of the doors were pulsing green and red. "That never happens."

The Roaming Wall drifted closer to the burning world. It was a blazing light of harsh warmth and winding coronal waves that jettisoned into the black void. Drade pulled their fortress vessel to rest upon one of these pulsing, looping tendrils and opened the soul gates.

The green flow of souls seeped from the fortress like a sieve and spilled into the coronal conduit. Emerald life force blended with the amber fury and followed the conduit back into the churning surface of the star, to the afterlife.

"It's beautiful," Seria said. "Are all souls meant to end their journey in the paradise within a star?"

Drade stood by her at the opening of the main gate. "All souls have the potential to fuel their home star. They are provided a place of safety and joy to live out the rest of existence, and in turn their power breathes life into the worlds that inhabit their system. It is as things should be; reciprocal, warm, joyful. That was the plan, at least."

"Whose plan?"

Drade shrugged. "Whatever made the Sun Guardians. Whatever it is, though, as powerful as it must be, it is no match for the vicissitudes of life. Some souls are deemed unworthy of the cycle, marred by evil deeds or a lack of good ones. They are rejected and roam the dark void to be preyed upon, which then fuels more violence against the living from Voir. It makes no sense for one so powerful to maintain such cruel, inefficient ways. And then there are the souls that are lost through no fault of their own." Drade breathed harshly through gritted teeth.

"Then why do you serve them?" Seria asked. "What catastrophe brought you into the Knights Cosmic?" Drade didn't answer. The pulses of the flaring star reflected off his translucent, technicoloured armour with a burning thrum. "... Captain?"

"It was the only way I could find to . . ." He didn't finish the thought; instead he breathed deep and let his shoulders sag. "It was the only way to ensure I could keep a promise, and even then, I failed."

"What promise?"

The green hue of the soul flow ceased, to be replaced by the pure amber warmth of the star.

"That I would always be strong enough to save the next person."

Seria understood now why his armour still raged. "I'm sorry," she said.

"Don't be. It was my fault she died," Drade said.

The silence stretched between them, punctuated by the droning thrum of the star. Then Seria finally built up the courage to ask, "The person you lost, was she your wife?"

A loud, dull tone echoed throughout the Roaming Wall.

"That tone sounded from Leppin's watchtower, on the bottom of the Wall!" Drade turned from Seria and stormed through to the Common Nexus. Seria struggled to keep up with him. "Summon your armour, Knight!" He ducked through a door and took a spiralling staircase down into the depths of the Star Fort.

Seria tried to still her fretting mind as Leppin sounded another low, ominous tone from the warning bell. She dug deep to find her fury, and found it fleeting. "Fuck." Still, she charged down the steps after her captain.

Halfway down the spiralling stone staircase, she stumbled as a wave of vertigo passed over her. She was still powering down the stairs, but it seemed to her that she was now travelling *upwards*. The paradoxical nature threatened to tear her mind asunder when the door on the landing below—or, well, above?—opened and Drawg scurried out of it. He had summoned his armour over his serpentine features, creating a sleek, angular design. Due to the pointed nature of his helm, it was easy to tell which way he was looking. When he looked at her in greeting, the stairs reoriented themselves in her mind. She was now definitely marching *up* the stairs, even though she had not turned around.

"What the hell is going on?" she said, grabbing her head and steadying herself with her other hand on the wall.

"Heh," Drawg hissed a laugh, "in the void between worlds, there is no true up or down. The Star Fort's magic has reoriented you as we are now heading to the top of the *lower tower*. Fret not, water nymph; it takes some getting used to." He took her by the hand with his talons and guided Seria the rest of the way up the lower tower.

They emerged onto a lookout that jettisoned from the underside of the cascading, tiered crenulations of starlit stone. Leppin, Harahn, and Drade stood there—already in full plate armour—looking out to a colossal structure that emerged from the abyss into the sun's light.

"That's the Star Citadel!" Drawg gasped.

"The Knights Council has come to us!" Leppin grinned through his open visor.

"No." Drade gripped the railing with quivering hands. "It's in ruins. Prepare for battle."

It took the remainder of the day for the Citadel and the Roaming Wall to sail within boarding distance. Not that the passing of a day mattered. The sun was still close by, pulsing with brilliant amber fire. It seemed to face them, Seria thought;

the sun had *turned* so that the so-called Sun Guardians could witness this strange event.

But she was sure that was her imagination.

Their Roaming Wall was huge by all accounts, but even it was dwarfed by the sheer size of the Citadel.

Their *little* Star Fort drifted over the plaza of the gargantuan, floating Citadel. The plaza was a vast paved courtyard decorated with an array of alien plants. It jettisoned out from the body of the Citadel like a welcoming landing platform. Only it was dark, the lamp lights inert, and it was marred by signs of great conflict. The watchtower protruding from the bottom of the Roaming Wall was inverted compared to the Citadel, so the knights now looked up at the courtyard as if it was a ceiling.

"Seria," Drade growled, "your armour."

"I'm trying!"

Seria tried to channel that fire. Sweat poured from her like flowing water. The feeling of water she understood, not fire, which she now needed. The only time she understood and channelled fire was when she witnessed the obliteration of innocent souls.

"Then I can't risk you going in with us," Drade said, placing his hand on her shoulder. "This is nothing to be ashamed of, but you are not yet ready to face what even the Council failed to quell."

"But . . ."

"But nothing! I will not lose more members of my squadron needlessly."

Seria faltered. The star-forged spear in her unarmoured hands seemed to wane in her grip.

"Fret not, little nymph," Drawg hissed. "You're only a new knight. It takes a while for a hatchling's scales to harden."

"Stand watch, Sir Seria Wish," Drade ordered. He stared at her through his visor, his eyes hard with the fury he was channelling, but dulled by his soft intent. "You'll be our backup."

"Aye," Harahn laughed, "I'll see a worm down there and scream in fright. Ignore that, and wait for two screams before charging in to save us."

Leppin and Harahn laughed, and the four knights launched from the watchtower—leaving Seria on her own as they soared on pillars of Prismatic Fire. Halfway between the Citadel and the Star Fort, they flipped over so that when they landed, they were oriented properly.

Seria watched sullenly as they marched with caution across the courtyard, up the steps, and through large, blue, steel doors into the Citadel proper.

"Knight." Drawg pointed to a dim, dull-armoured body within the entrance hall.

The hall was dim too, marred by gouged starlit stone on the floors and ceiling from conflict; furniture was overthrown, and blood and viscera lined the surfaces.

Harahn marched to the inert corpse and crouched over it. "Sir Nurol," he grunted. "She was captain of the Citadel's forces."

"So she, too, was denied her soul's honour," Drade said evenly. "Move on, into the Council chamber."

The four knights marched on, through the entrance hall and up a wide flight of stone stairs that were flanked by titanic pillars reaching into the imperceptible ceiling. Between the pillars were open passageways to other rooms, starlit by wide-open windows on either side and in equal ruin compared to the rest of the structure. A sinister clicking permeated the area, a sound like shards of ice breaking and sliding over eaves to strike hard ground. It was accompanied by the slow squelch of viscous stuff sliding over gravel.

"Voir," Leppin said.

"There must be many to make such noise," Harahn said as they reached the top of the stairs and found the Council chamber doors. They were thick oak and adorned with embossed gold and platinum patterns depicting the Sun Guardians and Knights Cosmic in alliance.

"No." Drade scanned the adjacent gloomy corridors, deep in thought. "There's just one Voir here right now."

"How could it make such noise?" Harahn wondered.

"Because it's enormous." Drade turned back to his squadron. "Open the doors."

Harahn nodded and barged through the door into the Council chamber, and what they saw made them freeze in horror.

Seria paced the watchtower and bit her nails, looking over the once-magnanimous superstructure of the Citadel—now a titanic, derelict corpse. The knights had been in there for a while now, with no signs of movement, until . . .

A colossal wormlike creature slithered out from crumbling crenulations, its gelatinous mass spilling onto the courtyard plaza with a sickening squelch. Seria gasped and ducked behind the wall of the lookout. It was a Voir, twice, maybe three times as big as the monstrosity that had attacked her city on her world. It wriggled across the courtyard, aided by the pull of hundreds of spindly legs and leaving a putrescent trail of grime in its wake. The featureless head perked up, looking at the Roaming Wall and Seria with an eyeless gaze.

Its circular mouth gaped and closed, sucking at the void between them.

Seria tried to steady her rattling heart, tried to take a full breath of air, tried to focus on her fury and summon her armour, but to no avail. She was simply too terrified, and there was no one in danger to save this time—other than herself . . . She was not as good a motivator for her Prismatic Fire as she would like to be.

She huddled into a ball and waited for it to attack, to launch itself through the ether and to smash her watchtower to bits. But no attack came. Cautiously, she craned her neck to look over the battlement. The hideous Voir gaped back at her, its impossible stare drifting between the Roaming Wall and some point out in space. Seria dared to follow its gaze, and her heart fluttered with relief. It was another Star Fort.

Only as it drew closer, it was clearly just as damaged and decrepit as the Citadel was. It drifted down to the courtyard—right-way up—and hung over the pavers with a dainty grace that did not match the bulky structure. The Voir writhed out of its way and reared to strike, but hesitated.

It's confused?

The drawbridge on the new Star Fort lowered, and a single knight strode out. A woman by the looks of it, a human woman, with a star-forged scimitar in tow.

The beastly Voir slithered down to regard the knight, bringing its insidious maw to bear, but it slowed. The new knight walked around it, more annoyed by its presence than anything. She stalked past the creature and up the entrance steps, disappearing into the structure unmolested. After a moment, the Voir curled over the edge of the courtyard and slithered out of sight on the other side of the Citadel.

"That knight." Seria rose from her hideout as she pieced the story together in her fear-addled mind. "If the portals weren't opening, if the Star Citadel had fallen . . . that could only mean there was a traitor in the knights' midst." Seria's fear dissipated like fog in the wind, replaced by kindling fury. "That knight is a traitor, there's no other explanation, and my comrades won't have any idea. They're walking into a trap!"

The kindling ignited, and she allowed the paradoxical sensation of flowing flame to run throughout her body and soul. It ignited out of the pores of her skin and solidified as pulsing Prismatic Armour.

The star-forged spear relaxed into her fingers, and she launched from the watchtower on a pillar of fire, hurtling for the imposter, hurtling to save her squadron, to save Drade.

"Sir Boln!"

Drade rushed from the doors into the ruined Council chamber, over which their commander was hoisted by the wrists on sinewy cords. His armour was cracked open, his fur and skin had been peeled back—he had been tortured—and his head hung low with blood dripping out of his lion's maw.

"Are you alive?" Drade leaped onto the star map table, his feet sloshing through the arcane waters as he took his leader's face in his hands, stroking fingers through his mane.

Boln's head lolled to one side, mumbling incoherently.

"Many of these portals are smashed." Leppin was circling around the long map table as Harahn took the other side and Drawg guarded the door.

"I see slime trails going through most of them. Yuck." Leppin scraped the underside of his boot on a chair, trying to remove some of the gooey material he had just squelched over. "The Star Forts were attacked from the inside . . . from here."

Drade glanced around the high chamber, finding the cracked and inert bodies of one other commander and the knight general. Boln's brother—Sir Rorc, who Drade had carried in not days ago—was discarded by the wayside.

"There should be a third body," Drade said as he cut Boln's bindings and lowered him gently into the water. "Stay with me, Boln, stay with me."

"I won't . . . betray . . . my knights," Boln whimpered.

"Shh." Drade stroked his mane. "It's okay, Commander, you didn't break." *I think.*

"No other bodies here; a bit of Voir stuff. There was quite a battle." Harahn grunted. "As far as I can tell, they poured through this portal." He gestured to one that was slightly less damaged than the others.

"That one leads to our Star Fort," Leppin said. "Drade . . . you were the last one to use it."

Drade snapped a look at the portal, wondering.

"It was not Drade." Boln coughed, spluttering blood and bile, which clung to his fur. "Sorcerer, a sorcerer hijacked your conduit as you left." His words were muffled.

"Sir Boln, do you know where you are?" Drade asked.

"Yes, what will soon be my tomb." He smiled weakly, revealing bleeding gums and cracked or missing teeth.

"Gods . . ." Drawg stepped over. "What did they do to you?"

"He tried to make me send a message to all surviving knights, have them congregate far away from the coming incursion . . . Once the Voir had a foothold, they would be unstoppable."

"Who tried?" Drade still stroked his mentor's mane.

"The gargoyle . . ." Boln's eyes widened with the word, but quickly relaxed. "He tried to control my mind, but I resisted. So he resolved to use more crude means. If he really wanted to break me, he would have shaved my mane." The lion knight laughed, but the weak sound was soon replaced by pained gasps. "Don't know where he is. Drade, he's imbuing the Voir with necromancy of some kind, letting them siphon the dead souls even after they take physical form. There is no limit to how large they can become."

"That's not right," Drade said. "Voir are mindless beasts, carrion feeders searching for drifting souls, nothing more."

"He has tamed them. Drade, his necromancy has been cast over us all. Kill him, and the knights whose souls should be escorted to the sun worlds will have their honour . . . They're still bound to their armour. They have not been consumed, yet."

"How do you know all of this?" Drade asked.

"When he tried to take my mind, he used pressure points, emotional triggers . . . There was some truth to his promises. He said he would free my brother from his armour. But I saw his promises for the manipulations they were. He would never uphold them." Boln reached up and grabbed Drade's helm with surprising strength. "Don't trust him, Drade. He will worm into your mind—you must resist."

"Okay." Drade gently pried Boln's paws from his helm. "But we need to get you out of here."

"No, my time is done. Drade, you must stop the gargoyle, stop the Voir, before it's too late."

"Where will they be?"

"Trist."

Drade's spine grew cold, the world where everything changed for him.

"Don't let your past control you," Boln murmured, his eyes rolling back into his head.

"I won't, Sir Boln . . ." Drade pulled a dagger from his boot. "Rest now, Lion Knight." He jammed the blade into Boln's heart.

Boln cried out weakly, but his suffering ceased, and his body went limp.

Leppin, Harahn, and Drawg stood tall and saluted their commander.

"So," they rounded on a new voice from the doorway, "if it isn't the upstart knight."

"Commander Shrath." Drade drew the words from his lips as if he had drawn blood from stone. "You survived." His grip tightened on the blade in his hands, the one dripping with his commander's blood.

"Aye, I fled as the Voir poured through the portal you opened," Shrath hissed.

"It was not him." Harahn stepped between the table and Shrath. "Boln just said that the gargoyle cast magic to splice himself into the conduit. Perhaps that is something you would understand if you had fought and died alongside your comrades."

"Hmm." Shrath shrugged. "In any case, there is work to be done. My squadron barely fended off the enemy as they breached our Star Fort. I came here to send out a warning to all other knights."

A warning sounded deep within Drade's mind. But he was still gripping the body of his saviour and mentor. He lowered Boln gracefully into the waters and stepped off the table. "Where is this magic that will allow you to communicate with all Knights Cosmic? I would like to be the one to send out the warning."

Shrath laughed. "You are only a captain. If you were to access the magic, it would only let you speak to your own knights. Only a general or a commander can speak to all within the order."

"Then I shall escort you," Drade said. "You never know where the enemy may attack next."

Shrath stared Drade down, her clear blue eyes battling with the stoic, cascading visage of his captain's helm. "Very well, your knights should guard the entrance hall, in case any other enemies are about."

Drade turned to his knights and nodded. They filtered out of the room and into the entrance hall as Shrath gestured down a side passage. “This way, noble knight.”

Drade gestured for her to go first, and she acquiesced.

Seria landed upon the courtyard with a clank and swore. She crouched low behind a fungus-like shrub and listened for the beast that writhed around the underside of the Citadel. The hissing, scuttling motion did not shift or change. She was undetected, for the moment.

So she leaped near silently from shrub to shrub, landing with squelching plops as she squished moist bodies or trod over soft petals. It was a danger that her armour felt so light and granted such power to her movements; she had to resist the ease of motion and the raging fury she was channelling in order to sneak to the entrance hall with minimal sound.

By the time she reached the hall—with one last leap and an assisting burst of Prismatic Fire—she found three of her comrades reacting defensively to her entry.

“Seria?” Harahn chuffed. “Your armour is shining bright!”

“Where is she?” Seria cried, a little too loudly. “The commander knight, where did she go? Where is Drade?”

“Commander Shrath? She and Drade are heading to a room that communicates with all knights. Why?”

“Because there’s a big fuck-off Voir wriggling around out there, and it let her pass!” She jerked her thumb over her shoulder.

The slinking, chitinous motion intensified as something loomed in the outer windows and burst through the stony portals with a screeching roar. The enormous Voir filled the room and reared to strike down at them.

Drawg leaped into action first. He sped under the creature's insidious legs and slid as he slashed up with his blade, tearing a ghastly rend in the putrid flesh that spilled white guts and mucus from its innards.

The smell was similar to rotting fish carcasses on the shore . . . Seria swallowed the vomit that inevitably emerged, and it burned her throat on the way back down.

"We'll deal with the Voir!" Leppin leaped high on a burst of Prismatic Flame and struck the creature's head. It flinched from the blow and swatted him from the air with a mass of limbs.

"Warn the captain!" Harahn bellowed as he charged in with his battle axe.

Seria nodded and sped from the entrance hall, tearing deep into the Citadel through random corridors that shone dully with waning starlight in the stone. The battle raged behind her, with thundering impacts sending granules of rubble falling from the ceiling on her path. The shuddering crashes were accompanied by the cries of her comrades and the hideous shrieking of the monstrous Voir.

"Where the hell am I going?" Seria fretted as she tore down the hallways and decided to let her fury guide her.

Some corridors were lit with more speckled light than others. She decided to take that as a sign that the Prismatic Fire was guiding her, or the Sun Guardians, or that she was terrified and wanted to stick to the brighter corridors. It did not really matter. She would search every inch of this accursed place to save Drade if she had to.

The rumbling crash gave Drade and Shrath pause as they entered the crystal chamber.

"Your knights have found the enemy," Shrath said. "We better make this quick." She strode into the room.

It was a hexagonal chamber lined with black stone; each corner sported a pillar of star-forged metal that pulsed like the throbbing of a heart. Against the far wall of the chamber was a dais with a perfectly formed orb of crystal placed upon it. It danced with nebulous light.

Shrath swung the door half open and strode in. It groaned shut after her, and Drade had to bar it with his free arm as he followed her in.

"So, how does this work?" he asked, restless angst creeping into his voice.

"Well, the crystal orb ignites with Prismatic Fire at the touch of a commander or general of the order. Once that is done, all knights, no matter how far flung across the cosmos, will hear the voice of any who places their hands on the orb."

"Good, now tell them to get to Trist, and we . . ." Drade quieted, all the hairs on his skin standing on end.

"What is wrong, Sir Knight?" Shrath placed her hands on the orb, which flared with stellar brilliance.

"That rasping . . ." Drade spun and brought his weapon to bear on the space on the other side of the door, but found nothing.

"Perceptive, for a frontline brute." Shrath chuckled.

"But not perceptive enough!" The rasping voice came from the ceiling.

Drade brought his weapon up to guard against the intruder, finding a hideous winged beast hanging by its foot claws, the gargoyle.

As Drade readied to battle the enemy above, he did not notice Shrath had charged him from in front. She propelled herself forward on pillars of Prismatic Fire, ready to skewer the exposed chest of Drade as his attention was drawn upwards.

From outside the chamber, there was a flash of Prismatic Light in challenge to Shrath's. Seria charged in, thrusting with her spear between Drade's arm and side to pierce the traitor.

Shrath cursed, ducked, and rolled. She slammed through the walls, her momentum was so great, and she tumbled through the empty hallways of the Citadel.

Drade ducked the other way, dragging Seria along with him, as the gargoyle conjured an amber flame in his claws to smite them.

"That knight is a traitor!" Seria yelled, froth boiling unseen under her helm at the corners of her mouth. "She did this!"

The gargoyle spread its terrible wings and descended on them; with a battering blow it knocked Seria aside and dug its claws into Drade's armour. The armour resisted the obsidian talons with a celestial screeching. Drade bellowed in defiance and grabbed his enemy's wrists, wrenching and slamming him into the wall.

"Make sure Shrath doesn't lead our knights astray!" Drade ordered. "Pursue her and keep her from the orb. I will deal with this devil!"

Seria stumbled to her feet without a word and grabbed her spear, launching after Shrath through the hole she had made in the wall.

Drade turned on his enemy, who stood, dusting off his wings and staring back at the knight with lifeless black eyes.

"Captain," its voice was like a rolling earthquake, "I was not expecting such resistance from you."

"Who are you?" Drade circled around the gargoyle, placing himself between it and the orb.

"I am Vurrel Maym," he hissed. Then he splayed his claws, and they sparked with amber flame. "And I am the sorcerer that will break the Knights Cosmic!"

"I have treated with sorcerers before. You will fall like all the rest."

"Aye, perhaps, but you have never fought one such as me!" Vurrel snarled and leaped, splaying his wings and summoning a mighty torrent that threatened to launch Drade against the far wall.

In response, Drade flourished his sword and embedded it in the ground, gripping onto it to anchor him in place. That's when Vurrel leaped for a high tackle, slamming into Drade's neck with his wing's shoulder and all the considerable weight behind it. Drade made a guttural sound and fell back, losing grip of his blade as he was driven into the ground.

Vurrel pinned him in place with his foot claws and rose to his full height, towering over the human knight. He raised his muscular, stone-like limbs into the air and conjured a pulsing cloud of red and yellow power. With a roar he slammed the spell into Drade's pinned form. Drade's cosmic armour flared in protest, but waned, cracking at the seams and letting some of the foul power channel into his flesh, causing him to writhe in pain.

"You are strong," Vurrel said, conjuring another ball of sorcery, and then another, to slam into the helpless Drade. "But even a stone must succumb to constant rain eventually. I am not the rain, though, little knight, I AM THE HURRICANE!" Vurrel spread his wings and conjured wind and lightning into the room as he channelled a colossal ball of sorcery above him. "My purpose shall be fulfilled!"

Drade summoned what fury he could—which was much—but he could not dislodge his attacker. He gritted his teeth in a set snarl and waited for the final blow to come.

Seria slammed into Shrath before she could right herself and flourish her curved scimitar around to bear on the enraged water nymph. Seria drove her shoulder into the traitor, and they crashed through another wall, sprawling out across a large chamber . . . the Council room.

"What's this?" Shrath picked herself up and danced around the inert portals as Seria tore after her with wild thrusts and swings from her spear. "A water nymph? What are you going to do, splash me?"

Seria retorted with a wail of rage, Shrath's taunting cry adding to her fury. With a blast of blinding light, she broke through one of the portal supports and swiped with her spear. It bludgeoned Shrath in the side and sent her tumbling again.

Shrath reacted quickly, rolling out of a stumble and swiping at Seria's legs as she tried to press the advantage. Seria copped the blade in her knee joint and collapsed on that leg, only halting from falling over completely by bracing on her spear like a staff. Shrath flourished her scimitar and made to lop Seria's head off, aiming for the chink in the armour between the helm and pauldron.

Seria gasped and focused on her innate ability, morphing her flesh into water form. Despite her raging Prismatic Fire, her body responded in time, and the blade passed through her neck as if cutting through a waterfall. Seria reformed a moment later, unharmed.

Shrath swore and faltered back as Seria lunged forward, driving her spear into Shrath's chest plate. The translucent armour dulled with a spark and crackle when the spear tip dug in and caught. Using the caught spear as a driving force, Seria rammed the helpless Shrath into the star map table. As the traitorous commander was slammed into it, the waters within the rim sloshed, sending dancing starlight across the dim blue room.

Seria wrenched the spear free and whirled it around to strike another blow, but Shrath recovered quickly—despite having the wind knocked from her—and dashed under Seria's reach. She whacked Seria's helm with the flat of her scimitar blade, sending a dull, disorienting ring that reverberated within the nymph's skull. Seria cursed and faltered, too distracted to morph her form into water as Shrath then slashed at the chink in her armour at the elbow.

Another concussive blow to the faltering Seria and another swipe to another chink in her armour had her on the defensive. She receded on the back foot. Each successive swipe from Shrath added to her rage, but not to her Prismatic Fire. This was frustration, not righteous fury. She could not calm her mind enough and focus in order to channel her Fire or let her water powers flow. Shrath had found her weakness, broken her fighting style, and now pressed the advantage.

The one-sided bout travelled down the star map table towards the balcony exit on the far side of the room. The eternal celestial night beckoned with dancing stars watching the warriors do battle. As they reached table's end, Seria suffered another blow and gripped the table for support; that's when Shrath spun and hook-kicked her across the face. The force of the blow was enough to send Seria over the corner of the table, ending up sprawled on the stone ground by the balcony's beckoning opening. She reached for her spear in a daze to find it was not within her reach.

Shrath laughed and leaped onto the table, sloshing through the waters and holding Seria's dropped spear aloft in victory. "This spear was too grand a weapon for a water rat like you!"

Seria spat blood over the inside of her faceplate. She was broken, bleeding, and turned to face her fate.

The Voir screeched as Harahn stabbed its head from a high perch. It reared and slammed him into the ceiling—sending him falling to the ground—while Drawg and Leppin swooped in and hacked at its legs and belly. It was withering under their constant attacks and would soon fall.

Harahn recovered from his fall, channelled Prismatic Fire into the plate of his arm, and launched up to strike the creature in the head with a mighty blow from his axe . . .

The gargoyle Vurrel made to slam his finishing spell into the defenceless Drade, but the ceiling collapsed on him at the last moment. The three Knights Cosmic dispatched the terrible Voir and sent its withering corpse barrelling through the Citadel. Vurrel was half crushed under the collapse, only one of his wings shielding him from death as his spell dissipated on the ground next to Drade.

Drade wriggled out of the gargoyle's half-buried clutch and crawled for the orb. He had to get some kind of message out.

He reached out with fingertips, about to caress the clear, crystalline surface that danced with starlight . . .

Vurrel bellowed, "No!" The gargoyle reached out with his claw even as the roof threatened to bury him, and conjured more crimson magic that shot straight into Drade's heart. "You will OBEY me!"

Drade screamed. The magic tried to dominate his will, breaking down his walls, overrunning core memories and goals and wants and desires, and settling on one deep, dark, hidden secret that even Drade was surprised he possessed.

With tears streaming down his face, Drade screamed in defiance. The will to give in to that dark impulse was all-consuming. His fingers touched the orb in his madness, and he was connected to the minds of his squadron . . . his team . . . his family.

Within an instant he overthrew the gargoyle's manipulative magic tendrils and gripped onto the orb fully. He could only talk to his own squadron; such was the way the knights were designed. That meant he could get hold of Rafek's and Arachton's minds . . . He told them with instantaneous thought what they had to do, despite the challenges they faced, and then the connection winked out.

Drade turned on the gargoyle, sword gripped in hand. "You will not control me like you have done others, sorcerer."

"Oh Captain." Vurrel slipped out from the crumbling ruin, the dust cloud shrouding him from sight. "You have no idea how many more ways I can break your will." He spread his black, taloned claws and stepped forward to fight, but the other Knights Cosmic streaked into the room from the destroyed ceiling.

Vurrel cursed and knocked them back with a spell of blue lightning before launching himself out of the hole and tearing through the corridors to flee the overwhelming odds.

"So that was the enemy?" Leppin asked, panting.

But Drade was already stalking past him. "Seria is in danger!"

Shrath hefted the spear to throw it at the defeated water nymph and end her life. There was a commotion behind her—the Voir's body barrelling through several layers of ancient Citadel—and Shrath paused to look over her shoulder. The star-speckled water sloshed around her heels, wavering through planets and constellations, and that was all the time Seria needed.

She whirled her hand, taking control of the only water nearby—the star map's—and spun it into a whirlpool that gripped Shrath's feet, then her legs, then her hips. Seria spun her enemy and lifted Shrath from the table before she could even gasp, launching her through the balcony window to slam on the platform's rim with savage force.

Shrath was now splayed out on the floor, on the edge of eternity with the starlit abyss spread out before her.

Her Prismatic Plate was shattered and went inert. Through coughing and spluttering Shrath found herself bruised, bleeding, and broken from the cosmic-fuelled impact of the celestial waters commanded by a nymph.

She reached feebly for her sword, but it whipped out of her reach, flying into Seria's hands along with her spear. The magic of the Sun Guardians had finally abandoned the traitor.

"Why?" Seria stalked over to Shrath as the human crawled back to the edge of the balcony platform. "You are a Knight Cosmic. These people are your kin, your brothers and sisters, and you betrayed them; you betrayed the oath you took and those your leadership was meant to safeguard. Why?"

Shrath's voice was feeble, trembling. "The gargoyle whispered into my mind. He promised me that if I served him, he could bring my son back to me."

Seria hesitated, standing over the weeping woman. "What?"

"The gargoyle serves something, something that the Guardians fear. He told me that if we defeated them on his master's behalf . . . he told me my boy would live."

"And you believed him?"

"No! His magic spoke to my desires. I could not resist. No one could!"

Drade and his knights tore through the balcony to find Seria standing over Shrath. Shrath stood as their coming broke Seria's concentration.

"I know my treachery cannot be forgiven," Shrath said, "but I just needed someone to understand." She spread her arms and fell over the edge of the platform, descending into the eternal night of space.

"She killed herself?" Seria asked breathlessly.

"And not pleasantly either." Leppin whistled. "As soon as she falls past the magic barrier of the Citadel, her body will kind of . . . well, the void does things to ya."

"Drade!" Harahn came running out. "The gargoyle escaped! He took Shrath's Star Fort."

Drade nodded, stoic as always, but his armour wavered under the dark thoughts the gargoyle had unearthed. "The enemy has been forced to make their move. We need to get to Trist."

"What's at Trist?" Seria asked.

"If we fail, it will be the place the cosmos ends . . ."

Part V: My Little Star Knight

A derelict Star Fort drifted into the custody of a warm yellow star. The fort was in ruins, and crumbling, starlit stone hissed into the ether in its wake.

It came to rest in orbit around an unassuming—but vibrant—little world. Its sphere was mapped with vast oceans and great continents of many different biomes. The climate was as varied as the people who lived there.

If the current denizen of the crumbling Star Fort told you that he was here to experience the richness of that life, he would be telling you a half truth.

He was a servant not of evil, but of something far, far worse.

He was Vurrel Maym, a sorcerer and gargoyle of the Court of Eln—a once-great dynasty. Their hardened flocks passed through the fabric of the cosmos before The Dark broke them on a whim. And now Vurrel served the bane of his people.

He came to this little world for the life that was there, that was currently being ravaged by The War of the Damned, and he was here to reap what he sowed.

Vurrel strode out onto an observation platform atop the ruined fort. It was like a courtyard made from a slab of starlit stone that was exposed to the great void. The world spread out before him, and from a tiny cluster of islands on the night side, a torrent of green wisps seeped into the ether.

Vurrel smiled, revealing cruel, obsidian fangs. He drew his staff from beneath his cloak-like wings—a gnarled totem with a red gem ensnared in its head—and weaved his terrible magic. He directed the flood of released souls into the maws of the hidden predator in wait around the world, into the maws of a single, incorporeal Voir of unfathomable magnitude . . . And he laughed all the while.

Twenty Light-Years Away

Rafek and Arachton huddled against the top of the tunnel, standing upon the shoulders of their fellow Knights Cosmic, whose technicoloured light danced off the brown stone earth.

"Why did you have to use me as a base?" one of the knights said.

The knight was a gnome who stood no taller than Rafek's waist. The monkey knight's big boots were currently crushing down upon the poor gnome's shoulders.

"Ook ook." Rafek laughed in his typical dopey fashion. "You looked sturdiest out of your squadron, fellow knight." Rafek grunted as he tore more earth away from the tunnel's ceiling, which spilled onto the angry gnome.

"Never mind your discomfort," Arachton chattered to the gnome. "Have your fellows confirmed that my kin are withdrawn?"

"They have burrowed deep, spider thing," the centaur knight who supported Arachton said. "I have heard scattered reports of Voir in the depths, but nothing your people can't handle. It is the swarms digging through from above that we must fear."

"And that's what this plan is for." Rafek grunted as he dislodged more dirt. "If Drade's psychic warning was not a fever dream, then any surviving Knight Cosmic is outnumbered, wounded, or scattered away from the real threat."

"How can anything but what is happening right now be the real threat?" an elf knight said, looking down the dark corridors of the tunnel.

"That's what worries me." Rafek hummed. "We need to get to your crashed Star Fort and channel our power into it. Between us all we should have enough Fire to launch it from this world and into the stars. As we lift off, I'll open the soul gates. The scent of soul should be enough to draw the beasts up with us. Then we send the fort into the depths of space, drawing the bulk of the enemy away from the innocents here as we make our escape."

"Yes." The gnome was fidgeting now. "So you keep saying."

"It'll work!" Arachton hissed in defence of Rafek. "It has to."

"Here." Rafek wrenched a stone from the earth, and the ceiling fell onto the knights in a cascade of soil. Through the opening was a cracked stone floor. Rafek pushed through it and pulled himself up into a ruined cellar. "The Star Fort's lowest room; it seems to be somewhat intact."

The rest of the knights crawled up into the dim space after him, spread out, and searched for pathways and other tunnels in the crushed, ruined room.

"How does this work again?" the gnome knight asked.

"We get to the Common Nexus and summon our Fire into the ruins of the fort itself," Rafek said.

"Very well." The gnome led them up a crumbling stairwell and through a shattered door into a large chamber. The floor here was tilted and rendered almost useless with craters and jutting edges. The ceiling threatened to collapse at the slightest breeze. "This is the place."

"All right," Arachton said, "spread out and wait for Rafek's signal. This might draw attention."

The meagre group of knights spread throughout the all but annihilated Common Nexus, interspersed between the inert portals, doors, and gates. Rafek nodded, and they all focused on their inner power. Their armour flared bright, and iridescent flames wicked from their plating like river mists in the wind and seeped into the walls of the fort.

The structure rumbled, shifting, awakening. The knights started to breathe heavily, not just from the exertion, but from the emotions that rose with their call to power.

Rafek gritted his teeth, and sweat dripped through his fur and down his brow, stinging his eyes. Arachton was curling her legs, bundling up into a ball, and the gnome clenched her fists, trembling all over as she brimmed with fury.

The fort started to lift from the mountainside; dust and debris crumbled from the structure and fell . . . but then started drifting upwards, sideways, and in all other directions as the sacred powers took hold.

The pulsing, listing, floating, titanic structure would have been a sight to behold as it rose into the sky. But all those close enough to witness it would have already been consumed by the swarms of Voir.

"Just a little more," Rafek grunted.

From deep within the structure, there was a sound of screeching metal and a horrible shudder that filled the knights with dread.

"Was that . . ." the centaur started to say.

"It was the soul gates! They broke open!" the elf cried. "The Voir will scent the remnants of soul-stuff and swarm through here!"

"That was the plan!" Rafek countered. "Keep channelling your energy."

"It's too soon!" the centaur bellowed. "We'll be torn to shreds while we stand here meditating!"

"Hold, you bastards!" The gnome leaped onto an overturned table, her armour shining with such bright fire it was almost white. "This is the burden we bore willingly." The hideous screeching of the Voir rose upon the air currents that drifted through the levitating ruins. "Our enemy will be here soon, and I will draw them down into the crater. Monkey Knight, once the fortress is high enough, drop it on them."

"But . . ."

"I followed your plan; now follow mine!" The gnome knight dashed from the table and tore deeper into the Star Fort.

"Where is she going?" Arachton cried, curling into a tighter and tighter ball as she struggled to produce her Fire.

"She's gone to the soul gates," the centaur said. "She is going to soak herself in the remnant scent of a thousand souls and use it to draw the beasts to her."

"Stay focused!" Rafek was roaring, his voice wavering as heat and fury threatened to overwhelm him.

The air grew cold and thin as the fort rose further into the atmosphere, and would have caused the knights to grow dizzy if it were not for the magic in their armour. The magic of the Star Fort was so weak, it could not protect them from the thinning air as it usually would; all it could do was levitate at their command, drifting into the beginnings of eternity.

The Common Nexus danced with shadows and echoed with foul shrieks as Voir swarmed over the fort from outside and wormed into the cracks. Rafek swore. The knights were rooted to the spot, focusing on keeping the fort flying; they would be torn to bits.

As the swarm of monstrous beasts started to pour into the Nexus, a great white comet streaked through from the other direction, trailing wisps of green soul stuff. It was the gnome knight. The beasts shrieked hungrily and tore after her, following the soul scent and breaking from the fort to descend into the cratered mountain range below.

"Rafek!" Arachton cried. "I can't keep this up!"

"HOLD!" Rafek ordered.

He broke a hold of his charging stance and stumbled to the gateway. He peered over the edge of the fort to find the brown-hued world spread out beneath him like a giant orb. Down upon the mountains, he sighted the churning swarm of thousands of Voir vying for the great light in the centre that thwarted them in their droves. The gnome would not last long.

With a heavy heart, Rafek turned back to the Common Nexus and bellowed the order, "BREAK OFF!"

With gasps, the remaining knights broke their focus and flew out the gate past Rafek, who stayed rooted to the spot long enough to make sure everyone got out. He held fast even as the fort started its return journey back to the mountainside, and his stomach lurched. As Arachton flew past him, Rafek jumped back out of the gate, and the rest of the ruined fort sailed past him, streaking towards the battlefield.

The knights watched in silence as the rest of their home crumbled and spurted flames, breaking through the atmosphere before crashing into the mountainside a second time. But this time it crushed the hungry Voir underneath it—as well as the brave gnome knight—in a colossal explosion of Prismatic Fire that streaked and ricocheted off the atmosphere like a rolling aurora.

"Will your kin be safe?" the elf knight asked Arachton, who watched the spectacle with morbid wonder.

"They burrowed deepwards and outwards; they will be fine. They can return to the surface soon enough. Your comrade, though, the gnome—what was her name?"

"Glrorin," the centaur answered.

"A fitting name," Rafek said quietly. "She gave her life not only for us, but the good people down there and all the other people who are now threatened in the cosmos. Come, we must rally our brothers and sisters and sail for Trist."

The Roaming Wall drifted within range of a pulsing yellow star, Trist's star. The stars that soared past them in transit had settled into their local constellations as they slowed down.

As they passed the threshold into the star's domain, into its arcane ebbs and flows, Drade suppressed a shiver. He had not been back here since . . .

"Captain." Seria touched his arm. They stood in the open gate of the Roaming Wall, along with the other members of Pride Squadron.

"I'm all right, Seria," Drade said. "Just old ghosts."

"You haven't been the same since your run-in with the gargoyle," Leppin said. "What did his magic do to you?"

Drade squeezed his fists until Prismatic Flame sparked and layered him in his translucent plate armour. "The magic showed me my weaknesses. I have stamped them out."

"Drade . . ." Seria started.

"Don't."

The knights bit their tongues and summoned their own armour as they came within sight of the world Trist. A world where in eons past all the races of the cosmos came together in peace and harmony for a time . . . until conflict brewed. The old portals were dispelled, and the species and races that contributed to the tapestry of life split into separate threads. Except for here, where most races held out against all odds.

"Fellow Star Fort sighted." Harahn pointed to a grey speck orbiting around the little blue world; it was arching towards them.

"By the Sun Guardians . . ." Drawg hissed.

As the other Star Fort orbited into view, so did a stream of green and crimson magic that broke upon Trist's atmosphere. It was the gargoyle's magic, necromantic power mixed with perverse sorcery. But that was not what made the knights gasp.

Between the orbiting fortress and the world, writhing within the magic, was a titanic, wriggling Voir. It was larger than the Star Forts, larger than the Citadel even, perhaps larger than an entire city. It writhed in abhorrent ecstasy as it siphoned off a stream of thousands—no, millions—of souls that flared up from the little world.

Harahn paled. "How can there be so much death on that world? Has there been some disaster?"

"War," Drade said. "The world is at war."

"But no war could possibly produce enough death for so many souls to . . ."

"The gargoyle has been pulling strings for a long time, using his necromantic powers to aid the Voir in their growth, using his sorcery to control them, to control us. I would wager that his trickery extends down to Trist's surface," Drade explained.

Drade motioned and the Roaming Wall halted by Trist's moon. He rose and soared out of the fortress upon technicoloured jets that burst from his boots. His knights followed, five warriors fuelled by star magic against the greatest threat the cosmos has ever witnessed.

As they came closer to the other Star Fort, they sighted their enemy. He waited upon the upper lookout of the structure. His imposing shale stone figure stood in stark contrast to the dancing blue and silver speckle of the Star Fort he had commandeered.

He now wielded a great, gnarled staff, which he whirled in wide arcs while beating his mighty wings to conjure magic. The magic siphoned the souls that tried to flee from the titanic creature into its very maw. It grew with every soul that was flung into oblivion within its endless belly.

"We have to stop this!" Seria cried. The fury struck deep within her, flame and water coursing against one another in a horrid, chaotic battle.

"If we attack the Voir directly, Vurrel will keep siphoning souls directly into it. If we attack Vurrel, the beast will be free to descend onto the world's surface," Drade cautioned. "We must divide our forces."

"But, Drade," Drawg growled, "the five of us cannot hope to defeat the Voir, let alone if we split up."

"You once told me that five Knights Cosmic could stand against any force in the cosmos!" Seria said.

"Yeah, but," Drawg gestured to the titan, "I didn't know *that* was a force that existed."

Seria drifted over to Drawg and slapped him hard across the helm. "Gird your loins, Knight. We took an oath to defend lost souls, and we are *going* to uphold it." Seria turned to Leppin and Harahn, who watched in shock. "Do you two have anything to whinge about?"

"No ma'am." Leppin and Harahn hefted their weapons.

Seria turned to Drade. "I know you, Drade; you won't risk us against the gargoyle's magic. Keep him off our backs, and we'll rip the beast's innards out."

Drade stared at her for a long moment, then at his depleted squadron. "This may be the last we see each other, whether we achieve victory or not. It was the greatest pleasure in my life to have lived alongside you." He beat his sword hilt against his chest and, without waiting for their reply, soared towards his enemy, towards Vurrel.

Vurrel cackled as he watched Drade approach. "Welcome home, *Captain*." He weaved his insidious magic with gusto.

Drade did not slow down, streaking through the ether to strike at the gargoyle like a hurtling comet.

At the last moment Vurrel ducked, and Drade swiped through nothing but tendrils of latent sorcery. He collapsed onto the Star Fort's platform, tumbling and sparking power as his cosmic plate scraped speckled stone.

Drade stopped tumbling and grated to a halt, scrambling to stand. The two faced off on the topmost observation platform of the Star fort. It was long and narrow and positioned to offer a prized view of Trist and the titanic Voir.

Vurrel stood at the edge of the platform, rearing to his full height—a head and shoulders taller than Drade. He spread his great wings and bore his staff like a holy relic in the hands of a pontificating priest with billowing dark robes.

Behind him, the blue-green world of Trist reflected the sunlight—silhouetting the malignant sorcerer. Without the funnelling of magic, the Voir now sought out the streaming green souls from the world's surface, which was streaked with gouges of fire and warfare.

Drade despaired at the sight, and Vurrel delighted at his anguish.

"Do you like what I've done with the place?" Vurrel asked.

"Not even if you bewitched all the minds of all the warriors on that world could you reap enough souls to feed that thing!" Drade pointed with his star-forged blade, the tip steady despite his brimming fury.

"Oh, but I didn't." The gargoyle laughed. It was a rolling sound that was like churning gravel. "I merely suggested to a few necromancers what they could really accomplish with their power. Over years I tended to their egos, until the strongest necromancers toiling in the heights of megalomania broke rank from their sacred duties and waged war against one another. They killed indiscriminately to forge hordes of ghouls for battle. Once the strongest prevailed, once the world was nothing but a dead husk whose surface writhed with souls entrapped in their corpses, I would descend to meet my successful pupils and execute them. The release of the souls all at once would fuel the glorious beastie you see before you. While I waited for my moment, I kept busy harvesting the souls from the minor conflicts around the cosmos. I created enough Voir to run you ragged for years!"

"So you have killed the whole world?" Drade started, pacing forward.

"Oh no." Vurrel stroked the amber orb on his staff with a black talon. "The War of the Damned was thwarted by a group of plucky heroes." He cackled. "But no matter, as you can see, the sheer amount of death that has already been wrought will be more than enough to slaughter your petty band of knights!" Vurrel launched into the air and swooped down on Drade.

Stone staff collided with star-forged blade, and man and gargoyle snarled at each other as they exchanged arcane forces in furious contest.

Seria found herself leading the flying wedge that tore across the void towards the titan creature. Drade did his job, distracting the gargoyle so that the souls were no longer siphoned directly into its circular maw. The creature searched around, coiling upon itself and clicking hideously as its gelatinous mass writhed and its spindly, irregular, deadwood limbs grated against one another.

Seria cursed the magic of her armour that allowed her to hear such a thing out here in the void.

The Voir made a bead for a stream of souls that tried to break around it, and Seria bellowed a battle roar, echoed by her comrades.

Almost perplexed—if a creature like this could experience such a feeling—it looked up as Seria rammed into it on Pillars of Prismatic Fire, thrusting her spear with fury. The tip of the star-forged metal drove deep into the thing's head before catching on chitinous matter. Seria lost her grip on the spear as it caught, and she slid forward, colliding into the abhorrent flesh with a squelch and ricocheting off its head in the other direction. Her spear remained behind, still imbedded in rancid flesh.

Harahn swooped in next, hacking with his mighty axe at a place where any sensible creature's neck would be. It cut a deep gouge, and the Voir keened in horrible pain before a stray limb batted the orc towards the world.

Leppin and Drawg struck in the next instant. The dwarf swooped and hacked away at the Voir's defending limbs. It struck back with the combined might of a dozen legs, but with a conjured shield of Prismatic Plate, Leppin blocked the reprisal blow. He was bludgeoned back as the tips of the creature's limbs splintered against his shield.

The Voir keened again, spreading its insidious circular maw to envelop the dwarf into a churning void of rows upon rows of razor teeth. But Drawg redirected his charge between Leppin and the maw, swiping and carving out a gouge in the creature's rotting gums.

It recoiled, writhing away from the two knights, only to find Harahn streaking up from the world to slam into its underbelly with another gouging flurry.

The Voir spun and flipped, fast—faster than a thing that size should be able to move—and tail whipped Harahn with a colossal snap that sounded like a thunderbolt.

Struck by something the size of a great river, Harahn's plate failed. The armour cracked and shattered, bones rendered, and organs ruptured. The dead orc tumbled through Trist's atmosphere, burning to a crisp within seconds.

Consumed by a rage that fuelled her power, Seria descended upon the beast from above, digging her newly claimed scimitar into its flesh and finding purchase. She stabbed and swiped and slashed—carving a way inside—intent on digging through the foul creature until she found a beating organ so she might tear it asunder.

The beast flopped around, snapping closed into a ball that encircled the ferocious water nymph. It squeezed her into a tiny compartment of horrid gelatinous folds and dead tree limbs. It started writhing again. The twisting, dragging limbs racked at her in a vortex of tearing blades. Every second that passed saw her assailed with dozens of tree trunk-like spears that meant to mince her to bits. She bit her lip and focused on her Prismatic Fire, conjuring heat and plate to keep the titan Voir from churning her into pulp.

From without, Leppin launched to strike at its head.

It reacted quickly and met him with a clump of pointed limbs. The defensive spike slammed into the streaking dwarf and pierced through his shield, breastplate, and heart with the sound of shattering glass. Leppin's Prismatic Fire winked out with a gasp, and the Voir tossed the now dull dwarf away.

Leppin's body tumbled limply through the ether.

Drawg hissed in fury and whizzed about the beast's head, harrying it with fast strikes. But it would not be distracted from pulverising the nymph within. Seria cried in anger, pain, and despair. The terrible weight crushed in on her from all sides; the horrible pain raked against her armour, and every crack and chip that was torn from it was a wound to her very soul. She focused on that, letting the pain fuel her fury. She could not give in; if she did, all of those souls from Trist would be consumed . . . a fate worse than death.

She tried to think; if she could focus, she could morph into water and slip away. But she would have to abandon her armour. The instant she did she would be killed by the Voir. Not to mention that cosmic magic would not protect her from the void if she was not actively conjuring it.

All she could do was brace and hold on for dear life.

Upon the observation platform, Drade crouched and swiped low at Vurrel's legs. Vurrel leaped high and flipped backwards over the attack. Seeing his enemy's exposed back above, Drade launched himself upon his Pillars of Fire to ram his blade into the gargoyle's spine. But Vurrel was ready for this; he twisted midair and battered Drade with his granite-like wings, knocking the knight into the ground with enough force to break stone.

Drade coughed—half winded—and struggled onto his hands and knees in time to dodge out of the path of Vurrel's spell. Snarling in frustration, the gargoyle strafed the area from above with fire and lightning. Drade danced around the fire bolts as best he could while copping lashes of lightning that strobed across his fluctuating armour.

With a roar, Drade tossed his sword. It flipped through the air—deflecting fire and lightning with its motion—before slamming into the gargoyle's staff. There was a blast of blue light, and Vurrel found himself hurtling into the ground amongst black smog and shards of wood and ruby. He hit the ground, and his own stone skin cracked and crumbled with the impact.

Wheezing through a crumbling neck, Vurrel peered through the smoke to see the bright lights of Drade's armour charging through the dimness. Vurrel gasped and stretched out his black-taloned hand, conjuring the sorcery of mind control. The spell struck Drade as amber flame, igniting his chest in brilliance as he staggered to a halt. The amber wisps and tendrils encircled his helm and dug into his eyes and ears.

"You have proven yourself an equal warrior, human, but you cannot resist my will."

"I have before!" Drade cried and stumbled forward. It was like forcing his way through thick mud. "Your will is weak!"

"Oh, but I have time to break you now. Look over yonder." Vurrel gestured to the battle with his other talon, which was stiff and cracked. "Your knights are losing. They won't be able to save you this time, and without them you'll have no foil against my persuasion."

Drade's heart fell, and his armour waned as he took in the scene. Harahn's death flared across Trist's sky, Seria was bound within a churning maelstrom of death, and Leppin was impaled and flung away. Drawg could not hope to defeat the titan Voir alone.

"Now," Vurrel's wheeze returned to its gravelly charm as his skin repaired itself, bit by bit, "you already want to betray the Sun Guardians, Captain. I feel the urge driving your rage. You want vengeance."

"Yes!" Drade cried, resisting the feelings that weren't quite his. "But not against them."

"Are you sure?" Vurrel twisted his talons and the amber magic dug deeper into Drade's mind. "Ah, I see. You hate them, but you blame yourself for that little incident . . . I would blame you too."

"Please, don't." Drade collapsed, his voice a whimper.

"Let's see, little Wundan Drade, just how weak you really are."

Drade screamed as he was catapulted back through time to the memory of his youth.

It was like he was there again, a small, helpless kid surrounded by death and smoke. His head was throbbing, his vision was wavering, but he could see everything clearly.

Mull—the bandit leader—tied his mother to the stake as his raiders piled oiled wood around it. Then he turned and tossed a small blade to little Wundan with a sneer.

"If you can beat me in a duel, I won't burn her," Mull said.

The other raiders laughed as little Wundan Drade picked up the knife and stood against his opponent. Mull stood three times as tall and twice as wide as Wundan, who felt the overwhelming urge to flee. But behind the bandit leader, his mother wept through her gag.

"Come on now, little rat," Mull taunted. "Come on!"

Wundan roared pitifully and charged forward. Mull mock gasped and sidestepped the attack before kicking the charging child over.

"He can do better than that!" a bandit jeered.

"Come on, kid, show him your mettle!"

Wundan stood again, and failed again. Each time his attacks became more desperate.

If only I was stronger.

The fifth time Wundan charged, Mull caught him by the knife arm and pummelled him in the face. Wundan fell back with a grunt and fresh pained tears in his eyes.

"Oh well, kid, I guess you didn't really love her." Mull shrugged with a sadistic smirk and nodded to his men.

With terrible laughing jeers they tossed their torches onto the pyre.

Wundan screamed as loud as his mother did and struggled to rush into the flames without hesitation. But Mull tackled him back into the ground, holding him in place for what felt like eternity. He held him there until the agonising business was done and his mother finally slumped forward on the pyre. The absence of her screams was a mercy, but it could only mean one thing.

"Now I want you to remember that, you little shit. You aren't strong enough to stand up to us!" Mull stomped on the sprawled Wundan for good measure before his band moved out of the dead, burning town.

Wundan Drade was pulled back into the present moment, full grown and screaming in absolute agony.

"Well, my! What a horrid little story," Vurrel chirped. "You weren't strong enough to save your mother, and you're not strong enough to save your squadron!" His voice turned hard again. "But if the Sun Guardians had sent the knights to your town *before* that Voir arrived to feast on your neighbours' souls, maybe they would have been in time to stop the raid." Vurrel cocked his head, tutting at the now whimpering knight before him. "If they actually cared about the lives they say they wish to protect, they would have stopped it from happening. They would have made you strong enough to stop it from happening. But *we* can correct that, Drade. Together, we can overthrow the bastards and usher in a new order, under the rule of one who has known their cruelty, one who will rule with strength. Join me, Drade, and you can get what you want!"

"But the souls!" Drade cried. "My knights! Your new order can't exist without their torment and oblivion!"

"A regrettable sacrifice," Vurrel nodded solemnly, "but *absolutely* necessary."

Drade doubled over, writhing in pain and agony, his armour strobing out of existence as his will and fury waned. He knew what was happening. He knew that the magic was trying to coerce him, making him want the unspeakable as it was offered to him. He had to fight it, to reject it, but how? He was utterly defeated. Even if he won over the gargoyle, his knights would still be dead, because he wasn't strong enough to save the people he cared about . . . again.

"I . . ." Drade whimpered, about to give in.

But something stopped him.

There was a streak of light across the battlefield, and a familiar booming bellow that echoed across the ether. "OOK OOK! I AM SIR RAFEK GAUNTLET! I AM THE MONKEY KNIGHT!"

Vurrel, Drade, and even the titanic Voir stopped to turn and look at the pulsing knight who had streaked into the fray. Rafek hovered in the void—splayed wide and proud—and bore a mighty war hammer of star-forged metal. Another streak came out of the cosmos beside him, producing a second knight, Arachton.

And then there was another streak of light, and another, a dozen, a score, a hundred more. The Knights Cosmic had gathered from the scattered corners of eternity. They had been betrayed, pushed to the brink of defeat, but were alive and filled with churning, righteous fury.

"Voir!" Rafek bellowed. "I challenge you! Time to drop the Gauntlet!" Rafek streaked across the battlefield, slamming into the Voir's head with a mighty blow from his war hammer.

The concussive force from the blow created a shockwave strong enough to ruffle Vurrel's stony, robe-like wings up on the observation platform. The Voir was knocked back, releasing Seria, who tumbled from the sharp, constricting innards of its coil. Drawg swooped in to assist her as the hundred knights soared forward on streaks of Prismatic Fire after Rafek's lead, swarming over the titanic Voir like a flood of light.

It reared and keened and shrieked in vicious contest, but the tide had turned.

Vurrel turned back to Drade with a look of fury. "No!" he spat desperately. "It does not matter how many knights you have; you will not be victorious. The Voir will destroy them all!

And you will serve me, Drade." Vurrel spoke quickly now, and the grating, stone-like nature of his panicked voice was like a crumbling fortress. "You can have what you want, *anything* you want, if only you serve the Whims of the Dark. Now tell me, what do you want?"

Vurrel's magic twisted into Drade's mind, showing visions of strength, of defeated Sun Guardians over a threshold of sunlight, and Drade's vindictive killing blow. But the vision was nothing compared to the fury of the Knights Cosmic that Drade now witnessed before his very eyes.

Fury, he remembered telling Seria, *a righteous rage, bent towards righting a wrong.*

"I want . . ." he stammered.

"Yes?" Vurrel leaned closer.

"I want . . ." Drade looked up, his armour manifesting completely once more as his fury—his *true* fury—flared. "I want to tear your fucking throat out!"

"What?" Vurrel flinched back.

Drade sprinted forward. Even with the pain of the magic, his wounds, and his emotional toll, he closed the distance between himself and his foe in an instant. He gripped the gargoyle's neck with both hands and wrenched. The crumbling stone skin faltered under Drade's renewed strength.

Vurrel gasped under the sudden force, his eyes straining as he was throttled to death, as his stone skin cracked and broke away. In desperation he tore at Drade's stomach with his obsidian talons, rending through even the Prismatic Plate and then raking through Drade's exposed gut.

Drade ignored the pain, because through the granular skin of the gargoyle's neck, he felt an artery, and he squeezed. Vurrel responded by tearing through Drade's exposed flesh and into his guts, grabbing intestines in taloned hands. Drade squeezed harder. Vurrel's black eyes rolled up into his head, but he still wrenched and pulled Drade's innards out from his torn belly.

Drade realised it would not be enough to squeeze the artery; he had to *rip* it from Vurrel's neck. He had to *tear* it from him.

Sensing Drade's intentions, Vurrel croaked one last desperate plea. "Without me, the magic of this fort fails." It was a pathetic, panicked wheeze. "Your armour is broken, your innards will be drawn from you into the void!"

Drade bit down on the bile in his mouth. "A regrettable sacrifice, but *absolutely* necessary!" He wrenched and ripped the artery clean out of the gargoyle's neck.

With a gasp, Vurrel's wings went into spasms and drooped as Drade—splattered in the gargoyle's purple blood—discarded his enemy. A pulse rippled throughout the fort as its master's magic abandoned it, and Drade was exposed to the void. His half-dislodged guts were ripped from his belly by the vacuum, jettisoning into the night.

Drade's armour still protected his chest, limbs, and head with its power. So he could still breathe and gasp in shocked pain as he collapsed to his knees. He sucked in a sporadic breath as his vision wavered, but instinct told him to follow the line of his entrails.

He looked past them and to the battle that still raged beyond. A dozen knights had fallen, but they had drawn the beast to extend itself fully, leaving it vulnerable to constant attack from every angle. Seria bravely flew across its skin, soaring through the forest of abhorrent limbs up to the head, where her spear still protruded from its flesh. She gripped it and called to Rafek, who streaked down to hammer it in like a nail.

With a flash of blinding technicoloured light, the spear drove into the Voir's skull.

The beast's cry was cut short as it went into spasms, and then it finally died and listed in the ether. The knights cheered when it wilted and the endangered souls flowed unmolested towards their sun.

Despite the pain and his fading vision, Drade smiled.

A warm light graced him, and his eyes turned to its source. A tall figure encased entirely in golden armour stood before him. It radiated warmth and golden light, with a towering solid gold crest upon its helm that was almost as tall as its body was.

"Captain." Its voice was deep, serene, and reverberated as if it was some colossus singing from the depths of the ocean.

"So the Guardians are free to escort the dead knights now?" Drade said, bewildered as to how he could still speak.

"Now that you have defeated the gargoyle's necromantic influence that bound their souls to their armour, yes."

The Guardian strode silently to stand beside Drade as they watched the celestial scene. Among the dead knights, there were other Guardians taking their souls and escorting them to their respective suns across the cosmos.

"I guess you'll be taking me now," Drade said.

"Perhaps. A war is coming, Captain . . ." The Guardian was interrupted when Drade laughed himself into a coughing fit, then continued, "We will need men like you at the helm."

"You mean lead the knights? I'm a soldier, not a general."

"It will be either you or Rafek." The Guardian tilted its head; the enormous crest loomed over Drade.

"Then make it Rafek; that'll bust his balls. Let me die. I just don't see why I should bother with it." Drade sagged.

"You have doubts about our purpose?"

"You know I do. And don't pretend you don't know I almost betrayed you . . ."

"But you didn't . . ."

Drade continued speaking as if the Guardian hadn't interrupted him. "And why bother with all of this effort, when you can just come in here and essentially resurrect me? Why can't you just stop this horror from the outset?"

The Guardian strode to the edge of the platform, looking out over the world of Trist. "I have often pondered this myself. The powers that be do not allow us to. They have not ever since my kind came into being."

"As far as I know, you *are* the powers that be. Don't give me that shit!" Drade's anger rose—not fury, but pure anger. "You could have saved everyone!"

The Guardian's head drooped. "Like in a dream, I have no recollection of when I began. I was simply there, doing the duty of a Sun Guardian. There was no life back then, just the stars we served that radiated their energy into the cosmos. But eventually, from that energy, life emerged . . . and died. As the souls from these first lives returned to the stars, they could shine brighter and create even more life. This has led me to one unavoidable conclusion, Drade. The powers that be, the real power we serve," the Guardian turned back to him, "is you."

"Me?"

"All of you, all life." The Guardian gestured broadly. "You are a product of the stars and a part of them at the same time. Whatever controls the process made it so we could not interfere with its own designs. We only tend to it. That's why we can give some measure of our power to paladins, but not intervene ourselves."

"I thought that Prismatic Fire was your power too?" Drade couldn't make sense of what he was hearing. He would be dead soon, though, so he figured it didn't really matter.

"No," the Guardian answered. "The Prismatic Fire is born in some souls that possess the will to safeguard the process."

"And what process is that? Huh? What's the point of all this suffering?"

"I believe," the Guardian paused, "all of this toil is so that you may discover it. Discover the struggle of purpose against an indifferent cosmos, a purpose that nurtures all souls to grow. I believe this toil is so that you may find the weight of joy. That you may feel it in the palm of your hands, to become that much richer for when you return home and provide that much more to the cosmos."

"Bullshit!" Drade spat blood. "There are so many horrible creatures! So much misery wrought upon the meek by monsters!"

"And those wretched souls are left to toil between stars when we discover their malice so that they may not contribute to the cycle, and that is what the Voir were for. They were supposed to snuff the malcontents from existence. It seems our enemy has weaponised their purpose against us. It is a good thing some souls possess the Prismatic Fire in order to fight them."

"But *she* suffered a terrible death!" Drade stumbled up and collapsed again, burying his head in his arms as he wept openly. "She didn't feel the weight of joy, only the burden of a pointless, painful death."

"Oh? Don't be fooled by a terrible end, human. Your mother also felt immeasurable joy."

The Guardian stepped forward and took Drade's face—now free of his helm—in its hands . . . in *her* hands.

"Wundan." Her voice was like warm honey.

Drade looked up into the Guardian's eyes and saw his mother. "Mum?" It was a wet choke of a word.

"Oh Wundan," she nuzzled into him, "you've been fighting again."

"M-mum?" Drade's eyes flooded, the tears streaming down his face as he choked back sobs and held her tightly. "Mum, I'm so sorry!"

"What for, honey?" She stroked his hair and cooed. "What for?"

"I couldn't save you, I wasn't strong enough, I let you burn!"

"Oh honey, you were just a kid, a kid standing up to a cruel, sadistic man. You were so brave, my little Star Knight."

Drade just shook his head and buried himself further into his mother's embrace. "I wasn't strong enough."

"You were so very strong, I was so scared you would not survive, but you did. And when that Voir crept into our village, when you stood your ground against it and conjured your armour at such a young age, you protected my soul from being consumed. I watched you battle it until that Lion Knight arrived. You did save me, Wundan. You were so, so strong. I'm so proud of you. Let go of your guilt. What happened was awful, but it was not because of you. Hush now, my brave little Star Knight. Hush." She kissed him on the head and pulled away.

Drade reached out for her, but his hands passed through the empty ether, and he instead found the Guardian standing in her place.

"Bring her back!"

"I broke cosmic law just to do that much."

"What does it matter if I'm about to die anyway?"

"Are you?"

Drade looked around at his entrails scattered about the void, jostling upon stellar winds like the tugging of spiderwebs. He looked at the dead knights as the Guardians escorted their souls; he looked at the withering, listing Voir and the army of knights that streaked towards him . . .

They needed him . . .

He was strong enough now.

"Fine," Drade spat.

The Guardian shone his light on Drade, and he found himself whole again, armoured and unhurt. Drade stood, relishing the feeling of painlessness, and strode past the Guardian as it started to fade from his sight.

"Prepare your knights as best you can, General Drade. The enemy—The Dark . . . it's out there. And it's coming."

"Before you go," Drade said calmly, "I have two things to say to you."

"Speak them." The image of the Guardian lingered.

"Take care of the knights who died, and make sure they get to their suns."

"It will be done, I swear." The Guardian bowed. "And the second thing?"

"If you ever step foot in my jurisdiction again, I'll break your fucking kneecaps."

The Guardian hummed, amused, and faded from sight.

"Drade!" Seria cried as she, Rafek, Arachton and Drawg soared towards him and halted over the platform, descending to embrace him.

"We thought you were dead!" Arachton hissed. "We could see the Sun Guardian's light."

"I told him to fuck off," Drade said.

"And he promoted you for it!" Rafek whistled. "Nice fancy armour and crest you have there, Drade." He gripped the crest and shook Drade's head while laughing in his ook ook manner.

"And the same to you, Commander," Drade said.

Rafek looked up at his crest and shoulder plates and swore. "Damn it!" They had morphed into that of a commander's.

"Don't do such a good job next time." Drade laughed. "Arachton, Seria, I am making both of you captains. You did so well. I am proud of you all."

"Captain . . . General." Seria nodded as her armour morphed and changed along with Arachton's. "I suppose this is just the beginning."

"That it is," Drade hummed.

"What is wrong, Drade?" Rafek grabbed him and held him close, a tight embrace that Drade returned, trembling as the emotions threatened to overwhelm him.

"I have been punishing myself a long time for deeds others committed. I am finally letting go, and I fear it will break me."

"Fret not, brother," Rafek said. "Countless times have you been strong on all of our behalf. Now our hearts can beat for yours while it mends from breaking."

Drade trembled, feeling silly and grateful at the same time. He did not pull away when his former squad huddled in and embraced him, under the watchful eye of the army of Knights Cosmic who floated in the ether.

"Okay," Drade said, feeling lighter than he had in an age. "I must address and organise the surviving knights. The Dark is stirring, and we must be ready to fight it . . . whatever it is."

A note from the author

Thanks for reading!

If you enjoyed this, please consider leaving a review. It helps people know this book is right for them, and is a huge help to me.

Do you want a FREE Sci Fi eBook?

Join my mailing list and I'll send you "Solar Rain" – *As one world burns, can a man stop his own from slipping away?*

Stay on the list long enough and you'll get sent free chapter samples to all of my available books, a free audio book of Solar Rain, and access to exclusive content in my newsletters.

You can sign up on my website https://seanmts.com[1]

My mission is to write kickass stories, with inspiring and relatable characters for all Sci-Fi and Fantasy readers to enjoy. I appreciate you coming along for the ride.

On my website you can browse my other books, check out my free fiction and read some spoiler free reviews.

If you ever want to get in contact, you can email me: sean@seanmts.com

You could also connect with me on social media:

Facebook: SeanMTShanahan

Instagram: @seanmtshanahan

Twitter: @seanmts

I am always keen to answer questions, or just have yarn.

All the best, may the Sun Guardians give you strength,

Sean M. T. Shanahan

---

1. https://seanmts.com/

About the Author

Sean works as a Tour Guide in Sydney, Australia. He has always enjoyed storytelling and considers himself to be a huge nerd, especially when it comes to Fantasy, Sci-Fi and History. The natural path from there was to combine those interests and write his own stories, which he started in 2015.

When he isn't scribbling down his whacky ideas or finding the worst pun in order to make his friends groan, he spends his time training for marathons or doing Parkour (in the hopes he will one day become an urban ninja).

Also by Sean M. T. Shanahan

The Science Myth Saga
Werewolves In Space
Dragon Roost On The Orbital Spire

The Symbicate
The Symbicate
The Symbicate 2 - Attack Of The Light Wizards
The Symbicate 3 - The Beast In The Void

The Whim-Dark Tales
Necromancing The Rose - Book 1 of the Whim-Dark Tales
The Daughter Of Darkness - Book 2 of the Whim-Dark Tales
The Weight Of Joy

Milton Keynes UK
Ingram Content Group UK Ltd.
UKHW020748231123
433129UK00017B/1102